"I'm no ladies' man, I admit," Ross said

"But if that's what you want, I can oblige."
And without warning, he pulled Vicky
into his arms and kissed her hard.

She was still recovering from the shock
when she felt his hand slip under her
blouse and start to caress her. Sheer fury
lent her the power to twist herself out of
his arms, and she glared at him while she
fought for composure, her cheeks and
heaving chest showing her indignation.

"Don't you ever touch me like that
again!" she spluttered. "You've bought
the station, but you haven't bought me!"

Not wanting to let him see how upset
she was, she swung away from him
and turned toward the door, but the
next minute found herself back in
his arms again.

JANE CORRIE
is also the author of these
Harlequin Romances

2020—RAINBOW FOR MEGAN
2038—SINCLAIR TERRITORY
2053—GREEN PADDOCKS
2072—THE BAHAMIAN PIRATE
2087—DANGEROUS ALLIANCE
2098—RIMMER'S WAY
2159—RAFFERTY'S LEGACY
2167—PATTERSON'S ISLAND
2194—THE TEXAN RANCHER
2209—PEACOCK'S WALK
2257—THE ISLAND BRIDE
2285—CARIBBEAN COCKTAIL
2313—THE SPANISH UNCLE
2335—TASMANIAN TANGLE
2365—THE STATION BOSS
2384—ISLAND FIESTA
2413—PIRATES' LAIR
2431—BRIDE FOR SALE

Many of these books are available at your local bookseller.

For a free catalog listing all titles currently available,
send your name and address to:

HARLEQUIN READER SERVICE
1440 South Priest Drive, Tempe, AZ 85281
Canadian address: Stratford, Ontario N5A 6W2

Ross's Girl

by

JANE CORRIE

Harlequin Books

TORONTO • NEW YORK • LOS ANGELES • LONDON
AMSTERDAM • PARIS • SYDNEY • HAMBURG
STOCKHOLM • ATHENS • TOKYO • MILAN

Original hardcover edition published in 1982
by Mills & Boon Limited

ISBN 0-373-02521-1

Harlequin Romance first edition January 1983

CHAPTER ONE

VICTORIA DALE sat on the paddock fence and surveyed the rolling pastures in front of her. The picture had always pleased her before, but now it had a sameness about it that made her long for new scenery.

A fly landed on her bare left leg and she sighed as she flicked it off. She didn't understand why she should feel this way. Dale's Creek was home to her, and she had been perfectly happy up until now, and she didn't see why she should let Cassy Brook's remarks get under her skin.

She gave another sigh. They were jealous, of course. Cassy and her friend Lucy Sean had had their eyes on Ross for years, and so had several other girls, she thought, and if it hadn't been for an understanding between Ross's family and Vicky's family that their marriage would amalgamate the two largest stations in the Albury district of New South Wales, Ross's life would be one continual siege of girls looking for a wealthy landowner husband, and add good looks and an easy disposition to the aforesaid, the tracks to Jarra Station would be strewn with casualties from the infighting to gain such a matrimonial prize.

The fly landed on her other knee and she flicked it off again. So they were jealous, she thought sourly, but the plain fact of the matter was that what they had said had been perfectly true, and it was that part of it that was causing her uneasiness. 'He wouldn't have looked twice at Vicky Dale if she hadn't been a Dale and only daughter of Gordon Dale,' Cassy had said, unaware that Vicky was sitting in a partitioned-off cubicle behind her in the teashop where she had gone to wait for her appointment for a hair-set in the adjoining salon. 'A man like that needs a real woman, not a skinny tomboy who doesn't look a day over sixteen,' she had declared emphatically.

Vicky was nineteen, and although she had no illusions about herself, she had been hurt by the reference to her age. As for being called a 'tomboy', she hadn't minded that at all; she was more at home in a blouse and jeans than a dress, and would much rather stay at home pleasing herself where she roamed on the huge sheep station that her father owned than pay the expected social calls whenever there was an occasion to go in to town.

Had Ross's mother been privileged to hear Cassy Brook's remarks, Vicky had a sneaking feeling that she would have agreed with them, but as both Ross's parents had died in an air crash two years ago while on a European tour, Vicky would never know the answer to that, but it was a fact that she had tried to bring out the feminine side of the girl they had nominated as their only son's wife in the not too distant future, and Vicky had found herself the victim of several stern if well meant lectures on the subject of genteel behaviour, and what young ladies did or didn't do, and that Vicky would pass on to her mother afterwards in satirical fashion, and her mother, after scolding her for not paying due attention to her lessons, would invariably be forced into a chuckle at her naughty daughter's mimicry.

The loss of Ross's parents only a year after Vicky's mother had died had brought them even closer together, although the families had been close friends for many years. Ross's father and Vicky's father had been firm friends since their boyhood and had grown up together. There had not been quite the same rapport between their wives, but certainly no dissent. Mrs Janson had done her best during that first difficult year for Vicky after she had lost her mother, but there had been such a wealth of difference in their views and upbringing, that it only produced a kind of resentment from Vicky, even though she knew Mrs Janson had her welfare at heart, for behind her well-meant interference Vicky had sensed a purposeful intention to groom her future daughter-in-law into the kind of wife she wanted for her son.

Mrs Janson had had high ideals, and were it not for the question of land, and the desirability of adding to their already substantial acreage, Vicky was sure that Ross's mother would have sought elsewhere for a bride for her son, for as the daughter of a wealthy auctioneer who owned a huge business that had branches in all the towns that dealt in wool and livestock, she had the right connections. She had also had the benefit of a good education, and it was this at times that had made Vicky's mother feel a little inferior to her, and not a little in awe of her, although Mrs Janson never consciously paraded the fact.

Vicky's thoughts then turned to Ross. What did he really think of the proposed match? Would he prefer to seek his own partner? What right had her parents, or his, to lay down the law as to who should marry whom? From the property angle it was a perfect match—and that, she thought crossly, had been their only consideration at the time, plus the fact that she got on with Ross, even if she was a little overawed by his autocratic ways.

She drew in a deep breath. What could Ross do about it if he didn't want to marry her? For all she knew he might have an undying passion for Ella Waden, the grazier's daughter whose station bordered Ross's on the south-west boundary, and whose beauty had awakened interest from most of the single men in the area without committing her to any one admirer. Waiting for Ross? she wondered. She drew in another deep breath. Now that would have to be a love match, for there was no question of gaining more land in that direction, as the station was under joint management with a city consortium.

Vicky's brown eyes narrowed against the glare of the sun. It was getting on for midday and she would soon have to go back to the house to prepare the meal, although she doubted if her father would be present. He had taken to making mysterious visits to the town lately on the slightest excuse available, and Vicky suspected that he was carrying on a surreptitious courtship that she would undoubtedly hear about when he was ready to tell her.

She stood up and turned slowly towards the homestead. Everyone, it seemed, was determined to keep her in the dark, not only her father with his newfound attraction that was keeping him away from his usual hawk-eyed watch over the station staff, but Ross as well, who had never bothered to talk over their future together. She straightened her slim back as she started back towards home. What it all boiled down to was that she knew nothing, she thought irritably. She had always accepted the fact that one day she would marry Ross, but had never bothered to examine the fact before, and now that she did, she was amazed at her feelings. Ross was like a big brother to her. There had been no endearing words, or even a sly kiss when they were alone, only a lecture if she did anything that he considered foolish, such as swimming in the Creek when it was swollen after a rainstorm and—oh, there were innumerable instances that she could recall, when his attitude towards her was one of forbearance rather than romance.

In point of fact, she thought sadly, romance simply didn't exist in the arrangement. As in days of old, that was something that came later—but would it? Her eyes widened as she imagined the future, and then she shook her head vehemently. It was all utterly impossible. She was very fond of Ross, but in a sisterly way only, the same as he felt about her, she was certain, but as things stood there was nothing he could do about it and he would go ahead with the marriage in due course of time.

She gave a slight shiver in spite of the heat around her as she envisaged their wedding night and the total embarrassment to both of them—not that she could imagine Ross ever being in such a state, he was much too sure of himself, but she would certainly be, and there was only one answer to that. Call the whole thing off as quickly as possible!

If Ross was so keen on adding to his property, then perhaps he could come to some arrangement with her father, which at that time would be no bad thing, Vicky mused thoughtfully, as she recalled her father's sudden loss of interest in the station. Only the day before Jake Loman had sought her out and reminded her to get her father to sign up the shearers for the following week as they were now on Ross's property, and usually made Dale's Creek their next stop, but as yet no firm arrangement had been made, and this was most unlike her father. They would come, of course, as they had come for years, but there were things that had to be arranged first, like moving the sheep down from the upper pastures and into the pens around the homestead. Jake, as foreman, would already have most of this organised, but he had to have Gordon Dale's go-ahead.

Vicky sighed as she entered the cool entrance of the homestead. She had never thought the day would come when her father would neglect his property to the extent that he had over these past few weeks. If it hadn't been for the vigilance of the staff everything would have come to a dead halt by now, Vicky thought.

As she moved into the lounge and on through to the kitchen, she found that her surmise that her father had not yet returned was correct, and she began to prepare herself a light salad lunch. While she ate her solitary meal, it occurred to her that her father might be contemplating giving up farming, and that meant that whoever the woman was, she was a townee, and had no intention of burying herself on a station, no matter how prosperous that station was.

When she had finished her meal she made herself a cup of coffee, and as she drank it her thoughts roamed on. She was certain that it was a woman who had caused her father's sudden loss of interest in the station. Nothing else made sense. Besides, all the signs were there. Her father's careful attention to his clothes, for instance. He had never been a man to fuss over his appearance, but things were different now, and it seemed a long time ago since he had looked Vicky in the eye without giving a sheepish grin and then making himself scarce over some detail that he ought to have seen to day ago.

Vicky was also sure that she was on the right lines over her guess that the woman was a town woman who preferred the bright lights of the city to the station plains, and she wondered if her father was contemplating settling in Canberra.

She gave a light shrug as she finished her coffee

and got up from the table and started to wash up her plates. Her father would tell her when he was good and ready, she supposed, when everything was finalised. The plain fact that he had not put her into the picture meant that he was not certain of his ground, and that he had not yet popped the question. He had not considered Vicky's future for the simple reason that her future was taken care of—at least he thought it was, she thought ironically. He did not know that Vicky was not going to marry Ross, she hadn't known herself until that morning, but this should not affect her father's affairs. If anything, it should make it easier for him, for he could then make an outright sale of the property at a price that Ross, who had inherited his grandfather's business, would not even miss from his bank account.

As Vicky laid the dishes on the draining board, she was amazed at her cool acceptance of the fact that if her surmises proved correct, she would soon be leaving her home and beginning a future that was entirely foreign to her. Perhaps she too would go to Canberra? She would not foist herself on her father and his new wife, as that would be most unfair, but at least she would be close enough to pay the occasional visit to them.

The prospect of a new future did not depress her, in fact, because of her restlessness that morning, it uplifted her. She would find something to do, she was sure, and there had been so much uncertainty hovering around her that she was glad of the chance of doing something positive.

She glanced quickly at the kitchen wall clock and saw that it was just after one o'clock. She ought to catch Ross at lunch if she left right away, she thought. That was the first positive step she had to get over with as soon as possible. It was no use hoping to catch him in the evenings, he was so immersed in the various local agricultural committees that if he hadn't a meeting at his place, he was out attending one at someone else's, and he wouldn't thank Vicky for barging in on one.

A few minutes later she was on her way to Jarra Station in her battered but much loved old Holden. As she neared the outskirts of the station, she could hear the shouts of the drovers as the sheep were herded into pens closer to the shearing sheds. All very familiar sounds, but for once it did not give her a sense of exhilaration, only an echo of the past that she felt was now outworn and over with as far as she was concerned.

When she neared the homestead, she saw with a sigh of exasperation that Ross was not where she had hoped he would be, having his lunch in the peace and solitude of the homestead kitchen, and where she had hoped to have a private word with him, but snatching a sandwich in between directing operations.

She drew in a deep breath. That was Ross all over, he had a good manager and experienced staff to cope with any situation, but he had to be in the thick of any activity. Once her father had been the same, she thought ironically, but times had changed.

For a moment she debated the wisdom of staying
and trying to get in a private word with him knowing that he would not be pleased by what he would
consider her untimely appearance in the smooth
running of the shearing operations, then she
shrugged her slim shoulders. Whatever time she
chose would be the wrong time, and she didn't
know what Ross would call the right time for such
a talk, not that he had any idea of what was on her
mind. Her smooth brow furrowed. Ought she to
put it off? she wondered, then her lips firmed in
resolution. It was now or never. If she left it to
tomorrow, she might not have the courage to carry
it through; there had been too much indecision in
her life—on her part anyway. She had just accepted
the plans that had been made for her future without
a thought of her own, and that went for Ross too,
she thought, and it wasn't good enough.

Encouraged by this thought, she got out of the
car and walked towards the shearing shed nearest
the homestead and where Ross stood issuing orders
from time to time and watching points with his
narrow blue gaze that missed nothing.

He did not miss Vicky's approach either, and
the instant, slightly exasperated look that passed
over his lean features was not missed by Vicky,
who should by now be accustomed to such greetings, but at that moment particularly resented it. It
was hardly the way one greeted one's beloved, was
it? she thought pithily, and if not beloved, the
woman he was going to marry!

None of this would have occurred to her a day

earlier, and she would have apologised to him for distracting him from his work, but things were different now, she thought ironically, and her soft lips twisted. Cassy Brook had been perfectly right about Ross's reason for marrying her, and would not have looked at her if it hadn't been for the acquisition of yet more land, and she suddenly wished that her father didn't own Dale's Creek and she could start from scratch like any other girl waiting for the right man to share her life with.

'Anything wrong?' Ross asked, as Vicky joined him, his vivid blue stare searching her face.

Vicky concealed her annoyance by fixing her large brown eyes on the pen next to the shed and absently noticing the way it was gradually being cleared of livestock, as the sheep were passing through to the shearing area. 'I want to talk to you,' she said, trying to inject an urgency into her words but knowing that Ross would be annoyed at her intrusion and was not likely to attach any importance to what she had to say.

'Can't it wait?' he replied impatiently, giving the answer Vicky knew he would give, then as another thought struck him he added, 'Is Gordon okay? I haven't seen much of him lately. I meant to call down the other evening, but something turned up.'

'Something', thought Vicky sourly, always 'turned up' with Ross, it was a wonder he found time to sleep. 'No,' she replied, 'Dad's all right. I just wanted to have a private word with you, that's all,' she added crossly.

'Well, I'm listening,' Ross replied, still with that

touch of impatience in his voice, and with his eyes
back to the sheep pen in front of him. 'Move the
next batch in,' he shouted out to one of the drovers,
making Vicky want to turn on her heel and leave
him to it, but the urgency that she had felt earlier
on the need to get this part of things over with
made her stand her ground and refuse to be
beaten.

'I'm not going to marry you, Ross,' she said
quickly before her courage deserted her. 'I've been
thinking things over, and I've decided it wouldn't
work. I just wanted you to know, that's all,' she
added on a low note.

For a moment or two it looked as if Ross hadn't
heard a word she had said, and that would be just
like him, too, she thought furiously, and if he
expected her to spend a lifetime talking to a stone
wall, then he had another think coming!

His blue gaze left the pen and rested on her
flushed angry face. 'Found someone else, have
you?' he asked softly, but with a hint of amusement
in his voice, as if he didn't believe a word of it.

'Of course I haven't!' Vicky replied indignantly,
and wished afterwards that she had said yes, that
would have shaken that complacent expression off
his face, but even while the thought was there, she
knew she wouldn't have got away with such a
barefaced lie. Ross knew her too well.

Ross's eyes went back to the sheep being herded
into the shed. 'Gordon's been spending a lot of
time in town lately, so I hear,' he said, in a matter-
of-fact voice. 'Guess you're lonely, huh?' he added,

with a lift of his autocratic brows.

Vicky's anger flared up again. In his eyes that would explain her extraordinary behaviour. She had wanted attention, so she had hit on a scheme of annoying Ross. So he hadn't believed her! Her hands clenched into small fists, and she wished she could hit him. He was so sure of himself.

'This has nothing to do with Father,' she exclaimed impatiently. 'And I'm not lonely. I'm used to my own company, as you very well know.' Her bright indignant eyes left him and settled on the sweeping pastures beyond the homestead. 'It's just that I got to thinking about us and—well, I guess I'd taken a lot for granted—never really thought about things, I mean. Now that I have, it——' she hesitated, 'well, it seems a ridiculous arrangement,' she ended firmly.

With his eyes, and Vicky suspected, his thoughts still on the busy scene in front of him, Ross said casually, 'And I've been kinda busy these last few months.'

'When aren't you?' Vicky retorted sarcastically. 'There's nothing new in that, is there? Look, don't you see. It's all very well having these arrangements made for us, but it's what we want that really counts, isn't it?' she demanded earnestly. 'We've been brainwashed into accepting the fact that one day we would marry, and it's just not on!' she added vehemently. 'It's not fair to you, and it's not fair to me,' she tacked on for good measure.

Ross's eyes studied her flushed features. 'That's how you see it, is it?' he queried mildly, 'And that's what you want?' he added, and gave a nonchalant shrug. 'Well, I guess that's okay by me,' and he turned his attention back to his stock, calling out to his foreman Jacko who had just appeared at the door of the shearing shed. 'At this rate we'll be through by this afternoon—better give Jake a call, they'll be ready to move on in the morning.'

Vicky's eyes were glinting as she stamped back to her car. She could have given Jake the message, couldn't she? she thought furiously, but she was only a girl, and station work was men's work. Ross took the same attitude as her father took, the woman's place was in the homestead, making things comfortable for the menfolk, she thought crossly, as she got in her car, and slammed the door shut, turned on the ignition and released the handbrake. She put her foot down with more force than was necessary and swinging the old car out of the homestead precincts headed for home.

If she was honest with herself, she would have admitted that her annoyance did not stem from the fact that the men in her life took such a protective attitude towards their womenfolk, but from sheer frustration at the calm way Ross had accepted her decision not to go ahead with their marriage.

It was as if, she mused darkly, as the car rattled along the uneven ground and over holes in the road that she would normally have taken great care to bypass, he had never had any intention of going through with it anyway, and was relieved that she felt the same way about things. It was almost as if she had made the whole thing up, she thought furiously, and he was grateful that she had come to her senses.

Her smooth brow furrowed as she recalled his vague-sounding excuse that he had been busy lately, and she couldn't think what that had to do with it. He had never gone out of his way to be nice to her, let alone court her, if that was what he had been hinting at, she thought satirically. Her soft lips twisted. She doubted if he knew the meaning of the word 'court'. He was married to his station, and she really couldn't see him going soft over a mere woman, and she pitied anyone who tried to alter that state of affairs. They would lose hands down.

Ahead of her she could see her home, a large sprawling timber and brick dwelling that nestled in the fertile slope of the valley, but even this view did not give her the usual sense of pride she had always felt when returning home. Oh, she needed a change right enough, she thought, as she neared the boundary entrance, and from where she could see that her father had returned. He had a way of closing the entrance gate that was almost a signature, jamming the steel framework tight up against the posts.

As Vicky closed the gate behind her and got back into the car, she wondered if this was the day when he would honour her with his confidences—and not before time, she thought grimly. It must be all of six to eight weeks since he had taken to sneaking off to town looking like a little boy who had just

found a lollipop tree and determined to keep its
whereabouts to himself in case he was denied the
treats in store.

Vicky sighed. She couldn't see Ross carrying on
in such a surreptitious way. Come to think of it,
there was a time when she couldn't see her father
doing so either. She drew in another deep breath.
There was a time for everything. She supposed that
one day even Ross, too, might succumb to the same
old fatal disease called love, but whoever worked
the oracle it certainly wouldn't be Victoria Dale!
Ella Waden, perhaps? She pulled the car into the
parking lot in front of the homestead. Well, there
was nothing to stop either of them now from going
ahead. Ross was going on for twenty-six, and it
was time he thought about settling down if he
wanted a son to follow in his footsteps.

Her father's Ford was parked in his usual spot
to the side of the house, and as Vicky walked into
the homestead she wondered if he had had his
lunch or whether he was waiting for her to rustle
something up for him, and her thoughts went towards the icebox and what she could produce in a
reasonably short time.

When she got to the living-room, however, and
saw her father slumped in his favourite old armchair staring morosely at a half finished glass of
whisky in his hand, all thought of food and other
mundane issues went out of her head, and she exclaimed, 'What's wrong?' in a low worried voice,
asking, yet sure of the answer. He had been turned
down, she thought, and wondered how she could

ease his obvious disappointment.

He stared up at her, and blinked as if startled by her appearance. He had been so lost in his thoughts that he had not heard her arrival, then he gave her a lopsided attempt at a grin, and Vicky wondered how much whisky he had had before her arrival. 'There's no fool like an old fool,' he said slowly, measuring his words, proving that he was not yet drunk but well on the way.

Vicky walked towards him and sat down opposite him. 'Turned you down, did she?' she asked softly.

Gordon Dale gave a hoarse chuckle that held no amusement in it. 'I guess that's one way of putting it,' he replied, then took a hearty swallow of his drink and drew himself up straighter in his chair. 'I got took to the cleaners, girl,' he declared harshly, and nodded at Vicky's astonished glance, and she was astonished. Her father had never been a gambler, he had much too much sense for that. He had never even betted on a local derby, calling it a mug's game.

'Gambling?' she exclaimed in a disbelieving voice. 'You?'

He shook his head as if to clear his senses. 'Ought to have seen it coming,' he said scathingly, 'but they were clever, I'll give them that much.'

Vicky got up from her chair as her father took another swallow from his glass. What he needed was good strong black coffee. She wasn't going to get any sense out of him in that state, she thought, and went through to the kitchen to make it.

After a lot of coaxing and scolding, Vicky won the day and managed to sober her father up, and bit by bit extracted the whole of it from him.

She learned that her earlier surmising of a woman in the background was right. Her father had met her at an auction in town. He had repeated his scathing comment of being an old fool and how he 'ought to have seen it coming', and then shaken his head and commented pithily that he had asked for all he'd got.

As Vicky listened, she realised the story had all the hallmarks of a confidence swindle. The woman must have been a very attractive person—but they were, of course. She was also a stranger, newly arrived in the town, which she would have to be to carry off the deception, Vicky mused, and supposed it was blackmail, she couldn't see what else it could be, and her thoughts turned immediately to Ross. Ross would know how to handle it, she thought confidently. 'How much is she asking?' she asked her father, thinking privately that the woman had a shock coming if she thought she was going to get away with it.

However, it was Vicky who received the shock. Her father stared at her, then cleared his throat. 'They've no need to ask,' he said harshly, 'they've got! They hold an I.O.U. that amounts to the value of the property.'

Vicky stared at him, unable to take in what he had said. Then she swallowed, and again her thoughts turned to Ross, and the sooner he was told all this, the better. Then her attention went back to what her father had just said. 'They?' she asked.

Her father nodded grimly. 'It was a set-up job,' he replied harshly. 'She took me to meet her brother——' he took a deep breath, 'at least she told me it was her brother,' he looked around for the whisky bottle, but Vicky was just that bit quicker and removed it firmly out of sight. He took another deep breath, before going on: 'He ran a hotel out on the outskirts of Canberra.' His lips twisted cynically. 'A casino, actually,' he added. 'I'm not so simple that I couldn't see that, but that was his business,' he shrugged, 'and Clarice didn't see any harm in it. She occasionally played herself—nothing big, of course, but enough to convince me that it was on the up-and-up.'

He stirred restlessly. 'You've got to hand it to them,' he said pithily, 'they knew they'd got hold of a silly old goat ripe for plucking. I'd played with small amounts from time to time, but last night,' he shook his head, 'I'd asked Clarice to marry me, and she said yes.' He ran a hand over his forehead. 'I guess I thought it was my lucky night, and splashed out a bit more lavishly on the tables. Of course, I kept on winning—if I'd lost earlier on, I'd have come to my senses.' His jaw hardened. 'So that's that,' he said finally. 'And there's nothing to be done about it. He's running a legal business out there, and as far as they're concerned it's the luck of the draw and I lost hands down.'

Vicky stared at her father, finding it hard to believe that he could have fallen for such an old trick as that, and if anyone else had told her the story she simply wouldn't have believed it. Again her thoughts turned to Ross. 'Ross—' she began.

Her father shook his head adamantly. 'Ross can't do anything,' he said firmly. 'He'll call me an old fool, and he's right. I'm only thankful that it can be kept in the family, because the debt's got to be paid. I'm looking to Ross for that, but as he'll get the station anyway in time, he'll see it as an investment.'

Vicky swallowed hard, and stared at the living-room carpet. Of all the times to tell her father that she was not going to marry Ross, this was hardly the best—but he had to know sooner or later. 'I'm not going to marry Ross,' she said slowly but firmly.

Her father's eyes, that had been looking longingly towards the cabinet where Vicky had replaced the whisky bottle, swivelled back to her in astonishment. 'Not going to marry Ross? Nonsense!' he said abruptly, then relaxed as if assured of his statement. 'Of course you'll marry him.' He shrugged offhandedly. 'You've fallen out with him, I suppose? Well, you'll make it up again. Storm in a teacup as usual,' he grumbled, and got up slowly. 'Guess I'd better go and see him and get it over with.'

'I mean it, Father. I'm not going to marry Ross. I told him so this morning and——' she hesitated, 'and if you want to know, I think he was relieved,' she added defiantly. She gave a half-rueful smile. 'In fact I know he was,' she tacked on, and moved across to where her father stood frozen in his tracks and laid a tentative hand on his arm. 'I'm sorry, Dad, but I wasn't to know about——' She left the rest of the sentence unfinished, but he knew what she meant.

'Not your fault, girl,' he said gruffly, and looked out of the windows towards the paddocks. 'This wants thinking about,' he said slowly, and walked back to his chair. 'Sure that Ross felt the same way about things, are you?' he asked her, and at her nod of confirmation, he gave a long sigh, and shook his head as if trying to dispel the fog that had settled around him. 'Guess I'll have to sell up, then,' he said grimly, 'and give him first offer. Can't see him letting it go elsewhere,' he added in a low voice, 'and I might as well get that over with straight away,' he commented bitterly as he got up, and jamming his stetson on his head marched out of the homestead, watched by an apprehensive Vicky.

CHAPTER TWO

GORDON DALE returned an hour later, and as she watched him walk towards the homestead after parking his car, she sensed a certain amount of relief in his step and bearing, and her own anxiety lessened and she threw a grateful thought towards Ross who had, as she had been sure he would, come to their rescue.

Her fine eyes met her father's thoughtful grey
ones as he entered the hall. 'All right?' she queried
softly.

Gordon Dale's mouth quirked at the corners
with some kind of emotion that Vicky could not
identify, then he said quietly, 'Better than I deserve.
At least we'll be able to stay on here. Ross is
coming up this evening to iron out the details.'
Then he gave a frown. 'I'd better put Jake into the
picture,' he added heavily, and went out again in
search of his foreman.

Vicky frowned. What did her father mean by
saying that they would be able to stay on? Of
course they would be staying on—where else could
they go? This was their home. Then she gave a
quick inward breath. It was not their station any
longer! Ross had agreed to buy the property to pay
her father's debt. She drew in another shaky
breath. Nothing was theirs. So much for her earlier
wish that she could be like any other girl who had
nothing else to offer the man in her life but her
love and devotion!

Her eyes widened as yet other thoughts entered
her mind, some of them not so palatable. How did
her father stand in all this? His pride had already
suffered a severe set back, and were there not more
to come? Now she understood that enigmatic look
of his. Couldn't Ross have lent him the money?
she thought indignantly. It wasn't as if he couldn't
afford it. As she remembered what had taken place
that morning, she gave a deep sigh. Had she still

been going to marry Ross this no doubt was what would have happened. As her father had said, it would have been kept in the family. She had chosen a fine time to declare her independence, she thought sadly.

Ross came after dinner that evening, and after giving Vicky an abstracted nod of greeting went into the study with her father, leaving Vicky feeling shut out and unwanted, yet it was her future too, wasn't it? she thought furiously, and she had a right to be present.

Her anger soon abated when she gave a thought to her father's position, and that whatever was decided he would not want his daughter present at such a discussion. There would be changes, not only in their status, but in the running of the station, for Ross had his own idea of management, and it did not always coincide with her father's.

An hour later the men emerged from the study, and Vicky, who had been keeping a sharp ear open for their emergence, flung down the magazine she had tried to interest herself in and rushed into the passage to meet them. 'Well?' she asked her father.

Gordon Dale looked at Ross as if to say, 'You tell her,' but Ross declined the obvious hint and gave an offhand shrug of his powerful shoulders. 'I've some figures to get out,' he said brusquely. 'See you tomorrow, Gordon.' With that almost casual dismissal of the pair of them, he walked out of the homestead.

Vicky felt a spurt of alarm. She hadn't liked the way Ross had thrown the ball back in her father's side of the court as if dissociating himself from the whole business. 'Well?' she asked again.

Her father took a deep breath before walking slowly over to his favourite chair beside the hearth, and after seating himself, started to light a cigarette. Closely watching his actions, Vicky saw that his hands were not steady, and she felt a spurt of sympathy for him. It could not have been easy for him. He had been made a fool of by a pair of confidence tricksters, and if that wasn't bad enough, he had lost everything he owned in the bargain. She walked over to the drinks cabinet and poured him a shot of whisky, and without a word handed it to him.

He acknowledged this action with a wry twist of his lips, but shot her a grateful look before he took a swallow from the glass. 'As I said before,' he began heavily, 'it's more than I deserve. Ross has bought the station. He's arranging to settle the debt with those bloodsuckers tomorrow.' He shot Vicky a quick half shameful look. 'He's putting Jake in as manager,' he said quietly, and added bitterly, 'suggested it was time I put myself on the retired list.' His hand holding the glass tightened. 'Guess I've not much choice in the matter.' He stared unseeingly at the old photographic print on the wall opposite him, and following his gaze, Vicky looked at it too. It was one of the first photographs of the old homestead soon after her father had taken over from his father. 'All for the best really,' he went on. 'My way's the old-fashioned way. Ross is all for progress. He offered me the figure work. Jake's got a lot to learn in that line—besides, it's not manager's work. Said I'll think about it, but I guess I'll accept. Being a station clerk is better than nothing, and I guess it will ease things for the staff too. That's the way Ross would have seen it.'

Vicky's small hands clenched by her side. How could Ross have treated her father like that? Why, it was like kicking a man when he was down! She thought of the station grapevine, and how soon the news would be broadcast from station to station. So much for friendship! she thought grimly. Surely it would be better if her father did retire. To stay on would only bring scorn and jeering fingers pointed at him. Station clerk indeed! 'Tell him to get lost!' she snapped furiously, and added indignantly, 'And to think I nearly married him! I was right to break it off. All he wanted was the station. He couldn't care less about us!' she fumed, and looked towards her father. 'Isn't there anything left?' she asked pleadingly. 'I mean, just enough for us to get out and live somewhere else? I could get some kind of a job in a riding stables somewhere—say, Sydney?' she suggested hopefully.

Her father shook his head. 'I wouldn't get anything at my age, girl. There's not much work around anywhere these days, and you couldn't support the pair of us. No, I'll take my medicine. If it hadn't been for Ross we'd be out on the street now.' He straightened his shoulders and patted Vicky's hand that she had placed on his arm as she made her entreaty. 'It's going to be all right.

Nothing will get out about the other business, that's between Ross and me. All the rest need to know is that I've decided to hand over the reins to Ross a little earlier than anticipated.'

Vicky nodded her head dumbly and went back into the kitchen to finish off the washing-up of their dinner things, a task she had put aside as soon as Ross had come, hoping to be included in the coming discussion.

When everything was stacked away, she slipped through to the hall and putting on her old thick cardigan, because the evenings were inclined to be chilly, she let herself out of the homestead. She knew her father would prefer to be alone to think things out, and come to terms with his altered status.

In a sense it was what she had to do too. It had never occurred to her that Ross might take advantage of her father's foolishness, for that was what she thought he had done. She didn't know how much he had paid for the station, but presumed it was more than the going price. Her smooth forehead creased. Was that why he had been, to her way of thinking, so hard on her father? She shook her head in silent disagreement with this theory. Ross was not like that, and it wasn't as if it had stripped him bare; he was an exceedingly wealthy man, and she couldn't see anyone getting the better of him in any financial transaction. He wasn't a man to haggle. It would be a case of 'take it or leave it' and under the circumstances, that precious pair of confidence tricksters would be only too pleased to grab what they could and move on in double quick time—Ross would see to that.

As she walked towards the paddocks, she heard the low bleating of the sheep in the pens waiting for the shearers the following morning. Her glance wandered on and over to the long hut, where she could faintly hear the murmurs of the men, who gathered there in the evenings, for a game of cards or just chat. They would have plenty to talk about tomorrow, she thought sourly, as she walked on.

The moon cast a sombre light on the property, showing gigantic shadows in the distance from the stately pines to the south of the station. Vicky drew in an inward breath. She felt incredibly sad, and it was nothing to do with her father's lapse from grace, but with the way Ross had handled the whole thing. Even though she was furious with him, she couldn't help feeling terribly let down. Ross was family, and though she wasn't going to marry him, he was still the one she would always look to for help in any awkward situation—or had been, she reminded herself sadly.

Now things were different. Ross was the station boss now. Things would be different all round. He didn't believe in half-measures. He had often said that the homestead needed modernising, and no doubt he would see to that too, she thought angrily, although it had been good enough for her and her father and suited their way of life. Whatever he wanted to do, he would do, and neither she nor her father would have a say in the matter.

She rested her elbows on the fence railing and

stared ahead of her. Somewhere there ought to be a sign stating that the station was under new management. Not that anyone would be under any delusions from that score. It was all very well her father thinking that everything would be hushed up, but he had forgotten that bad news travels fast, and there's always someone who knows something. His frequent visits into town, for instance, must have caused some speculation—his complete loss of interest in the station itself, even more.

She sighed. What it all amounted to was that she and her father were nothing more than hired help. Her brows went up at the thought. What exactly was she being paid for?—housekeeping? They owned nothing, so they would have to earn their keep. Her father had got his job lined up, but what about her? Her lips clamped together tightly. It was true that she did all that needed to be done about the homestead; perhaps she wasn't as efficient as Mrs George, Ross's housekeeper, but she did what was necessary, she told herself sternly, but a guilty conscience reminded her that she ought to have turned out the spare bedrooms long before now. Everything was tidy, but the rooms did need airing, a state of affairs the capable Mrs George would never have allowed to exist.

Her chin jutted out in a defiant gesture. If Ross dared to interfere with her way of doing things, then she would soon show him! Another sigh escaped her. What was the point? It wouldn't get her anywhere. The place was his now. She stared unseeingly at the shadowed landscape before her.

Just wait until she saw him! She would tell him exactly what she thought of him! Her father might feel obliged to stay on, but there was nothing to stop her leaving.

It wasn't, she argued silently to herself, as she made her way back to the homestead, as if she would be letting her father down. It wasn't as if he needed her support—in fact it might be better if she was off the scene for a while until things settled down again. She wouldn't go too far away, she thought; Albury would do nicely, and she could slip home for the occasional weekend.

Her thoughts raced on as she let herself into the homestead. Aunt May would put her up until she got something. She frowned as she took her cardigan off and hung it on the coat rack near the door. Her father wouldn't like that arrangement at all, but he'd prefer her to be there rather than with complete strangers, and now that Aunt May was safely married and no longer a threat to his peace of mind, Vicky could see no reason for his refusal, although he still wouldn't like it.

'Aunt May' was a courtesy title bestowed on Vicky's mother's best friend, a friendship that had lasted through their schooldays. Angela had married, but May had remained a spinster until a year ago, having finally given up all hope of becoming Gordon Dale's second wife, for the two girls had fallen in love with the same man, but Gordon had soon scotched any hope of May's in that direction by his determined courtship of Angela.

After Vicky's mother's death, Aunt May had
offered to come and housekeep for them, a not
altogether altruistic offer, though it meant her
giving up her small curio shop that catered mainly
for tourists. The offer had been politely but firmly
turned down, self-preservation coming to the fore
where Gordon Dale was concerned.

Vicky had attended May's wedding a year ago,
and had been pleased to find that the man she had
chosen was a kindly man, and not someone on the
lookout for a handsomely endowed middle-aged
spinster, for Roy Marks was an accountant and a
fairly successful one, handling the accounts of several prosperous wool men and in no need of hand-
outs from his new wife.

Up until her marriage Aunt May had lived above
the shop in a flat that was small but adequate for
her needs, and it was this flat that Vicky hoped to
be able to make her new home. Aunt May, now
Mrs Marks, moved out to her husband's home, a
large establishment on the edge of town, and in
keeping with her husband's prosperous vocation.

Vicky knew that the flat was now being used as
a storage area. Aunt May had told her that she
had never known where to put her stock before,
but now that the flat was empty she would have
ample space for storage, and had gone on to say
how happy she was that Mr Marks had put up no
objection to her keeping on her little business.

Full of her plans for the future, Vicky went in
search of her father to tell him of her decision to
move out, and steeling herself to the opposition

that was bound to come, but told herself that once he had slept on it, he would see the sense of her argument.

She eventually tracked him down in his study, lost in a welter of figure work, and her hopes rose as she surmised that he was trying to salvage something from what had been their property, enough perhaps for them both to leave?

At this point he looked up suddenly and saw her standing there. 'I could do with a sandwich,' he said, almost absentmindedly, before he settled back to his task.

Vicky smiled as she went back to the kitchen to fix him something. That was more like her father! He was a great one for his food—or had been, before he was led up the garden path by a couple of crooks.

As she cut the sandwiches and prepared a pot of coffee for him, she knew she would have to leave her news until the morning, and who knows, she thought cheerfully, if her father did come up with something he would have a few ideas of his own. Whatever they were, Vicky would go along with them, just as long as they could leave and not be beholden to Ross, who thought more of property than friendship.

To Vicky's intense disappointment, the following morning did not bring fruition of her cherished hopes of something being salvaged. Her father was very quiet during breakfast, not that he ever said a lot, but he only spoke when necessary, refusing a second helping of toast, and a third cup of coffee, a very bad sign to Vicky, who had hoped for better things. 'I guess Ross will be around soon,' he said heavily, as he got up from the table. 'I'd better see that Cooky's got enough rations in, the shearers started this morning.'

'Oh, Jake will have seen to that,' Vicky said easily, and at the wince this statement produced from her father wished she had thought before speaking, and began hastily to clear the table.

'Oh, sure, Jake's pretty competent,' her father replied, with a trace of bitterness in his voice as he left the dining area.

Damn! thought Vicky. That wasn't very tactful, and it really wasn't like her father to take things that way. He would have been the first to admit that Jake was a first-class foreman who did more than his fair share of work, more so since her father's distraction from work.

That settled it! Vicky thought grimly, as she almost threw the crockery into the washing up bowl. She would have to have things out with Ross. Her father was too proud to stand up for himself, and had meekly accepted the post Ross had offered him, and that in itself had been an insult. Clerical work! she fumed. A job for a retired man, who was well past the hard physical work of a station. Not that her father did any physical work now, but he did run the station, and surely he ought to have been offered the manager's job?

She took her frustration out on the job in hand, and the water splashed in all directions, but she was too incensed to feel the growing wet patch on the front of her cotton blouse that made it cling to her slim figure, outlining her small high breasts. Just wait until she saw Mr Ross Janson!

'Washing up or taking a bath?' queried an amused voice behind her, the voice of the very man she had wanted to see.

'What does it look like?' she demanded furiously, as she whirled round to face Ross. 'Where's Father?' she asked coldly. What she wanted to say to Ross was not for her father's ears.

His brows rose at her tone. 'Supervising the shearing at the moment,' he replied. 'Why?'

'Because I wanted to have things out with you,' Vicky said furiously, and added bitterly, 'I suppose he can manage that.'

Ross's blue eyes narrowed. 'Got in a right paddy, haven't you?' he said softly. 'I should leave that part of the business in the hands of the men. Gordon's not complaining,' he added complacently.

Vicky's furious eyes threw out sparks at this calm statement. 'How the devil could he complain?' she asked angrily. 'He was only too grateful to you for coming to his rescue. He had no choice but to accept what you offered him. I would have thought that he rated a bit higher than a desk clerk, though,' she spat out at him.

Ross's calm gaze rested for a moment on her flushed face and her small clenched hands from which the water dripped on to the kitchen floor, and he casually threw her a tea-towel. 'Get dried up,' he commented, and staring at her drenched blouse added, 'and change out of that wet blouse.'

Vicky's lips clenched together at this authoritative habit of his of ordering her around. 'It'll dry,' she said crossly, and jerked the clinging blouse away from her skin, but only succeeded in sending the small pearl button fastenings scattering and leaving her hastily clutching the ends of the blouse to preserve her dignity, 'Now look what you've done!' she exclaimed furiously. 'And don't change the subject. Why couldn't you have offered Dad the manager's job?' she demanded.

Ross's eyes were still on the blouse, but he recollected himself in time to reply haughtily, 'I had my reasons, which I may or may not tell you. I'll think about it,' he added infuriatingly, and gave a curt nod towards her state of undress. 'Do something about that first. If your father comes in now, we'll have to get married,' he stated with a wide grin that revealed his strong white teeth.

'Very funny!' Vicky snapped back at him, but she was hurt by his amusement. She knew her father would take no such attitude, to the pair of them she was still a little girl. Her wish that she had nothing to offer but herself had come true, she thought ruefully, but she had forgotten that a girl with no money did need a certain amount of good looks, and she ought to have wished for beauty to cushion the blow. Because she was hurt, she took refuge in sarcasm. 'Even Dad's not that dumb,' she said pithily. 'Romance isn't exactly your scene, is it?'

Ross's eyes narrowed to a slit, and Vicky felt a

spurt of gratification at having got through that calm exterior of his. 'I'll admit that I'm no ladies' man,' he said abruptly, 'but if that's what you want maybe I can oblige,' and without warning pulled the unsuspecting Vicky into his arms and kissed her hard.

She was still recovering from the shock when she felt his hand slip under her blouse and start to caress her. Sheer fury lent her the power to twist herself out of his arms, and she glared at him while she fought for composure, her bright cheeks and heaving chest showing her utter indignation. 'Don't you ever touch me like that again!' she managed to splutter out furiously. 'You've bought the station, but you haven't bought me. Go and find someone else to practise on—there are plenty who'll be only too happy to oblige you!' There were tears in her eyes as she said this, and not wanting to let him see how upset she was, she swung away from him and turned towards the door, but the next minute found herself back in his arms again and being treated to what she could only describe as a bear-hug.

She froze when she heard her father's voice behind her, and his somewhat embarrassed, 'It'll keep,' as he made a hasty exit again.

As soon as they were alone again Ross released her, and seemed to have recovered his good humour as he drawled, 'I told you to do something about that blouse, didn't I? I want a leisurely walk down the aisle, not a shotgun gallop!'

'I'm not walking down any aisle,' Vicky

managed to get out, 'and most certainly not with you!' she exclaimed, furiously tugging the two halves of her blouse together.

'Of course you are,' Ross said complacently. 'All we need is a bit of courting practice. I must say I liked our preliminary skirmish—come here,' he commanded loftily.

Vicky found the door with the instinct of a homing pigeon and raced for her room, slamming the door behind her. Although out of sight and earshot of Ross, she knew he was laughing, and again she experienced that odd sense of hurt, but that was at the back of her mind, overridden now, by a sense of shock.

Ross, of all people, she thought shakily. She was not ignorant of the wiles of men, but Ross would have been the last man she would have accredited such behaviour to. Did he no longer respect her? Was this the result of her altered status? She recalled the way he had made fun of her, using her disarrayed appearance as an excuse to manhandle her. So she had annoyed him by her cutting remarks on the lack of romance between them, but she hadn't asked for that.

She walked to the window and stood gazing out. As for his blithe statement that of course she would marry him—her brow darkened. If that was the type of courtship that he had in mind then no doubt she would marry him. Shame alone would make her take that trip down the aisle! Only the man you intended to marry should ever be that intimate, she thought, with a blush of recollection at his light yet searching touch. And he hadn't even apologised! she thought indignantly.

'Vicky!' her father's voice drifted up to her, cutting off her musings, and Vicky hastily searched out a T-shirt and changed out of her blouse, thinking as she threw it on the bed that it ought to have scorch marks on the front, and was vaguely surprised to find that it was still damp, considering her treatment at a certain person's hands!

CHAPTER THREE

WHEN Vicky got downstairs, she was relieved to find only her father there. She wasn't sure how she would have faced Ross. His abrupt change from his brotherlike attitude towards her to one of determined courtship was going to take some getting used to, and Vicky needed time for adjustment.

'Cooky could do with some help at smoko,' her father said as she joined him, and gave her a searching look. 'Made it up with Ross, have you?' he asked quietly.

Vicky shook her head. 'No,' she said abruptly, and as she felt the colour rise in her cheeks, she turned away from him and walked towards the door on her way to the cookhouse, before he saw her embarrassment.

'Then what was that little scene in aid of?' he asked persistently, before she could make her escape.

For a moment Vicky was at a loss for an answer.
If Ross hadn't made such a big scene out of it, she
could have explained the reason for his grabbing
her at that particular moment, but as things stood,
he wasn't likely to believe her. 'Oh, I think he was
annoyed because I wouldn't reconsider going
ahead with our engagement,' she said carefully. 'I
think he's trying to make up for lost time. We
weren't ever on that kind of relationship, were
we?' she went on quietly. 'That's why I called the
whole thing off. The truth is we're more like
brother and sister than an engaged couple.'

Her father thought this over for a second or two.
'He's a good catch, girl,' he said gruffly. 'There's
plenty waiting on the sidelines hoping he'll look
their way.'

'I don't want a "good catch",' Vicky said crossly.
'I want someone who really cares for me. It's
probably just that I hurt his pride in breaking off
the arrangement. You know how he likes his own
way.' She turned to face her father. 'Well, I ask
you—he's never done——' she hesitated here, and
willed herself not to blush, 'anything like that
before,' she added lamely, thinking it was a good
job her father didn't know the whole of it, for if he
did, Ross's amused comment of a shotgun wedding
would become a reality, of that she was sure.

Gordon Dale nodded his head. 'There might be
another reason,' he said slowly. 'It'll cause talk,
you know. He takes over the station, but doesn't
marry you. It won't take folk long to come up with
an answer to that one. It won't look too good for

Ross. Sure, he's highhanded and has a mind of his own, and if he's satisfied with the arrangement, he'll go ahead.' He paused for a second, then added, 'Guess I'm not too pleased with the way things have gone, but I've let things slip around here, and I had it coming, but he's a good man for all that. The way I see it, you'd be saving yourself a lot of trouble by just going along with him.'

Vicky's small chin jutted out, a sure sign to her father that she had other ideas. 'And that's a good enough reason, is it?' she demanded crossly. 'I should marry Ross simply because everyone expects me to? because of an old arrangement made years ago?' she declared pithily.

'It never worried you before,' her father said quietly.

Vicky's indignant eyes met her father's eyes, and she gave a small shrug. 'I'd never really thought about it before,' she said with a hint of an apology in her voice. 'It always seemed so far away——' Her voice trailed off, and she stared down at her sandals.

'Look, girl,' said her father gruffly, 'I've some idea of what's wrong. I guess it's partly Ross's fault, and I've not been much help lately, have I?' He passed a hand over his forehead. 'Your mother would have known what to say. It's sincerity that counts—and I ought to know,' he added, with a bitter twist of his mouth. 'So Ross isn't the hearts and flowers type—well, that sort of man flits from girl to girl like a bee collecting honey, and you wouldn't want a man like that for a husband, would you? If Ross isn't hung up on you, he certainly isn't hung up on anyone else—that's for sure. As long as you respect each other, all the rest will follow. All I'm saying is give him a chance.'

Vicky's eyes remained on her sandals. It all sounded so easy, she thought miserably, and she couldn't explain how she felt, not to her father. Her mother would have understood. She sighed inwardly. She would have to try to make him understand, for her and Ross's sake. Her fine eyes lifted to meet her father's. 'That's what I'm trying to do,' she said quietly. 'Give Ross a chance. Oh, not only Ross,' she added quickly, 'myself as well. You said there'll be talk if we don't marry, but you know what they'll really be thinking?' she demanded. 'They'll be nodding their heads and inwardly congratulating him on a wise decision. He's never had a chance to look around. At his age most men have flirted with several girls until they've found the right one.'

Her eyes went beyond her father and rested on a picture hanging on the passage wall. It was a landscaped painting of meadows and old oaks, and simply titled 'An English Landscape' and was a favourite picture of hers. It had a timelessness about it. It spoke of the past and the future. It was the future that Vicky was more concerned with now. 'I believe that there's someone special for everyone,' she said in a low voice. 'Sooner or later you meet that someone.' Her eyes left the picture and came back to her father. 'What happens when Ross or I meet that certain person?' she asked quietly. 'It's all very well saying that such a thing is unlikely. You met Mother, didn't you? How would you have felt if she hadn't been free to marry you?' she asked softly.

'That's different,' said her father impatiently.

'I don't see how,' Vicky replied. 'The trouble is, it's so easy to forget how it was at that time, and it's not convenient to remember, is it? Not when it doesn't suit. It's my life, Dad.' She gave a little shrug. 'If I went ahead and let Ross and you bully me into marriage I'd feel I'd cheated him and myself,' she shuddered. 'I can see the future. Ross making excuses for his absorption in the station with me sitting in that huge homestead of theirs wondering how to fill in my time.' She gave her father a half-amused, exasperated look. 'He's more out than in, isn't he?' she said scathingly, 'and my being his wife wouldn't make the slightest difference to him. I can't see him hurrying home with tender thoughts of keeping me company, can you?' she asked ironically. 'Not me, anyway—for the right person, yes.'

On this determined note, Vicky left for the cookhouse. She was certain that she hadn't managed to convince her father, or Ross, come to that, that she meant to stick to her word, and not be browbeaten into carrying out their respective parents' wishes just for the amalgamation of the two stations, which now had actually happened without the necessity of marriage.

Once in the cookhouse, Vicky pushed all these annoyances out of her mind. She loved shearing

time. The whole station took on an urgency that
transformed it. The drovers' shouts, the constant
cries of 'Keep 'em moving!' The endless supplies of
food and strong sweet tea at smoke time, accompanied by the constant blatant flattery from the
younger bloods of the shearing team, calculated to
produce a thicker slice of the puddeny cake they
were so partial to.

Only one remark marred the day for her, and
that was when one of the team rather overdid the
flattery, and received a good humoured rebuke
from the foreman. 'Easy on the blarney, lad. That's
Ross's girl you're chatting up, and we need his
business!'

Vicky then had to endure a lot of teasing, and
when was the wedding? remarks, and considering
what had taken place that morning she was in no
state to humour them, but did manage to hold her
tongue. People would know soon enough that there
wasn't going to be a wedding, but the remarks gave
her food for thought. She was used to being called
'Ross's girl', but there had been no mention of a
wedding before, and this worried her. She knew
that news travelled fast on a station, and it often
had nothing to do with the usual channels of com-
munication. All it required was a couple of station
hands with Aboriginal blood in their veins and who
had inherited the uncanny knack of 'knowing'.

So it was now common knowledge that Ross
owned Dale's Creek, she thought sourly, and sin-
cerely hoped that the whys and wherefores behind
his sudden acquisition of the station would not be

bandied abroad, and although this was unlikely, for all the hands were trustworthy men, she felt very uneasy. The only consolation was that she was still expected to marry Ross, and surely this was a good sign. They were expecting the wedding to take place in the near future, adhering to the old agreement between the two families, and that had been common knowledge for years.

However comforting this thought was, concerning her father's affairs, anyway, it was not so helpful for Vicky. It showed only too plainly that her father's comments that it would look bad for Ross if the marriage did not take place was a fact, and not a ruse to make her change her mind, as she had earlier suspected.

The way things were going, she thought irritably, as she walked back to the homestead in good time to prepare the dinner, she would have to marry Ross, in spite of her fine speech that morning when she told her father that she meant to give Ross a chance—a chance that he didn't seem to appreciate, she thought crossly, only because there was no room in his life for sentiment. His first and last love was for the land, and anything else would be dovetailed to fit in its allotted space. Everything, that was, but her, Ross was man enough to meet any criticism, and would soon plough through anyone who hoped to disconcert him by even as much as a hint in that direction. Ross, she decided, could well look after himself, and there was no need for her to worry on that score, for she had no intention of being pigeonholed into the role he had allotted her, even though it did mean becoming the wife of the State's largest station owner.

On going into the kitchen, Vicky noted with a sigh of exasperation that she had forgotten to take the lamb chops that she had planned they would have for their meal out of the freezer, and she stood wondering what else they could have at such short notice, and searching in the freezer, came up with meat patties. Their meals these days seemed to consist of last-minute preparations, for Vicky was no hand at cooking. To be fair, there had been a time when she had really tried to produce meals comparable to what her mother used to serve, but trying was as far as she had got, for it could not be said that she succeeded, and she had come to the conclusion that her talents must lie in other directions. Her father's absence from the evening meal during the last two months, had resulted in her not bothering to cook anything on a grand scale, but getting herself quick and easy meals when and if she was hungry.

This state of affairs was shortly to be put to rights, for Jake had told her that afternoon that Ross had suggested that he and Mary, his wife, should move into the homestead directly, as befitted his new position as manager, and at the time Vicky, who had not taken the news too well, even though Jake had assured her it would only be until Ross had fixed them up with permanent quarters on the station, had wondered sarcastically why Ross hadn't made it a permanent arrangement.

When she had got over her annoyance, she had to concede that this was an unworthy thought. She liked Jake, and she got on with Mary. Neither of them was likely to take advantage of Jake's new-found promotion, and, she suspected, had put up some opposition to the scheme when it was put to them by Ross. But Ross's 'suggestion' would have been an order, and seen as such, and therefore would be carried out.

After clearing away their evening meal, Vicky slipped up to the bedroom that Jake and Mary would be occupying the following evening, and saw that all was made ready for them. In her mother's time it had been the main guest bedroom, and in some small way would show Jake and Mary that they were welcome, in spite of her rather un-enthusiastic acceptance of the news from Jake earlier that day, and of which she was now ashamed, for her mother would have heartily approved of the arrangement; in the old days, Mary had helped in the homestead, and Mrs Dale had been very fond of her.

When she went back to the sitting-room to join her father, Vicky also conceded that having Jake around meant company for her father. They were both fond of a game of cards, and all in all, it should work out very well.

Her father would have been of the same mind, where Vicky was concerned. Mary would keep Vicky company, only Vicky had other ideas. As soon as it was possible she intended going ahead with her cherished scheme of moving out of Dale's

Creek, and getting herself a job, but first she had to get in touch with Aunt May, she reminded herself.

She had also, she thought guiltily, to tell her father, and there wouldn't be another opportunity after this evening, not with Jake and Mary around, she thought, as she settled down in her usual chair by the window and glanced across at her father browsing through some catalogues giving the latest price of fleece. 'I've put Jake and Mary in the front bedroom,' she said casually. 'It will seem odd having company after all this time, won't it?' she added conversationally.

Gordon Dale grunted an absentminded affirmative but continued to study the catalogue in his hand, and Vicky wondered if he had heard what she had said, but after a moment he lowered the catalogue and looked at her. 'Get on all right with Mary, don't you?' he asked. 'She's a good cook, too,' he added ruminatively.

Vicky's eyes widened. 'Thank you!' she said indignantly. 'I didn't think I was that bad!'

Her father grinned. 'Now I didn't say you were, did I? It's just that Mary's got a light hand with the pastry,' he added.

'So you kept telling me for a week after she'd sent over that steak pie a few months ago,' Vicky said dryly. 'It might just have been a one off success for all you know,' she added teasingly.

'Best cook on the station,' said her father. 'Everyone knows that. Even Cooky admits it, and he doesn't hand out compliments often.'

Vicky was glad that her father had got his appetite back and was looking forward to his meals, cooked of course by Mary. 'In other words, leave the cooking to Mary,' she said with a smile, and at her father's quick nod of confirmation she added, 'I'll be glad to. In fact, she'll have to take over anyway shortly.' She hesitated; now was the time to mention her plans for getting a job. 'I've decided to get myself a job,' she said casually, and before her father could interrupt, added hurriedly, 'I shall ask Aunt May if I can use the flat above the shop while I'm looking around.'

Her father stared at her. 'Ross won't like that,' he said emphatically, 'and I don't like it either. I don't know what's got into you—not going to marry Ross, and now all this talk about getting a job. What sort of a job, for goodness' sake?' and not waiting for an answer, he carried on, 'This is your home and it's where you belong, and that's how Ross will see it too, you mark my words!'

Vicky sighed. She had known it wouldn't be easy, but she hadn't expected her father to rely on Ross's co-operation in ganging up on her. 'It's got nothing to do with Ross,' she said impatiently. 'As for this being my home—well, it isn't now, is it?'

Her father's tight features told her that she ought to have chosen her words more carefully. 'I'm sorry, Dad,' she said quickly. 'I didn't mean it that way. I know you won't believe me, but I'd decided to get a job before that happened. When I told Ross that I wasn't going to marry him, he put it down to loneliness—said I'd been too much on my

own,' she gave a small smile. 'I suppose in a way
he was right. I was fed up with everything. I wanted
a change but didn't see what I could do about it—
not until—well, you know what,' she said, hastily
skimming over that part of it. 'I still didn't see how
I could leave, but then I heard about Jake and
Mary moving in with us and I knew you'd have
company. It's not as if I'm going far away,' she
added. 'I should be able to come home for week-
ends now and again. As for the job I shall get, I
shall have to wait and see what turns up. One
thing's certain, whatever it is, it will be a change
for me,' she declared firmly.

Her father said nothing, but his lips were tight
as he turned his attention back to his catalogue
again, making Vicky feel wretched, but she was
determined to stick to her resolution. Once Jake
and Mary were there, things would be different,
and he wouldn't even miss her, she thought con-
solingly.

To Vicky's disconcertion, Ross called shortly
after eight, and she found herself hoping that it
was a business visit and was not going to be a re-
petition of what had taken place that morning, but
when he settled down in the sitting room with
them, and made no attempt to talk business, she
knew it was a social call.

She also knew that she ought to feel flattered
that he had taken the trouble to keep them company, but she only felt a sense of annoyance. She
couldn't remember the last evening he had spent
with them. It was so long ago. The days of the

family gatherings had ended shortly after the death of his parents.

In all fairness, Vicky had to admit that Ross's father's sudden death had given him a lot of responsibility. Instead of a gradual takeover of the station, he had had to take full charge at a moment's notice, and considering the size of the station, this was no mean task. Being the type of man he was, he succeeded, and the station prospered, but at the cost of the close friendship between the families.

'I'm thinking of throwing a shindig for the shearing gang,' Ross said casually, as he stretched his long legs out and eased his lean frame into a more comfortable position in the deep armchair opposite Vicky's father's chair. 'They're throwing enough hints around,' he added with a grin.

Vicky looked up from the two-ply jumper she was knitting, and almost dropped a stitch. As long as that was all they were throwing hints out about, she thought darkly.

'Better get it organised while the girl's still around,' Gordon Dale said gruffly, and ignoring the accusing look Vicky sent him, went on, 'Got some daft idea of getting a job in Albury.'

Ross's expressive brows lifted and he stared at Vicky, who hastily turned her attention back to her knitting. 'Since when?' he asked softly.

'Don't ask me!' growled her father. 'She's no call to leave, and so I told her. Perhaps you can talk some sense into her,' he added as he got up, and collecting his catalogue, marched to the door.

'Think I'll see if Jake wants a hand in packing up,' he said, and refusing to meet Vicky's indignant eyes, left the room.

'So?' Ross asked softly.

'So—what?' Vicky replied crossly, determined not to be browbeaten by him.

'You know what,' Ross answered, still with that silky note in his voice that told Vicky that she was in for a lecture, and she resented it. 'What's this about a job?'

Vicky took a deep breath and put down her knitting. It was no good getting mad at him, and she supposed he had a right to know, for the old friendship between the families if nothing else. 'It's just an idea of mine,' she said patiently, 'and a good one. I need a change, and it's about time I struck out on my own,' she added firmly.

Ross continued to study her, his blue gaze going slowly over her slight figure. 'We could always bring the marriage plans forward,' he said carefully. 'There's no point in looking for work. Forget it.'

Vicky's blazing eyes met Ross's cool ones. 'I'm not going to forget it!' she blazed at him. 'I'm tired of being told what I should do and what I shouldn't! This time I'm pleasing myself—and I wish you would listen to what I say,' she added crossly. 'I said I was not going to marry you and you didn't listen, but I mean it. Look,' she said exasperatedly, keeping a wary eye on the firm set of Ross's jaw, 'things are different now, aren't they?'

Ross's brows lifted. 'How?' he queried loftily.

Vicky gave an impatient shrug of her slim shoulders. 'You know very well what I'm talking about,' she said accusingly. 'This station was-well, I suppose you could call it my dowry, wasn't it? Well, you had to buy the station, and that wasn't the idea at all, was it? It certainly wasn't the way your parents wanted it—mine either, come to that, but it's a fact, and you know something else?' she tacked on firmly, 'they wouldn't expect us to go ahead under those conditions. I mean, it's not as if we had an undying passion for each other, is it?' she demanded, adding hastily as she saw Ross rise slowly from his chair, 'and no amount of the kind of bear-hug you gave me this morning will alter that,' she declared. 'Can't you see I'm letting you off the hook?' she asked impatiently.

'I don't recall complaining,' Ross said dryly. 'As for all this talk about love——' his firm mouth twisted in an ironical sneer. 'It's overrated,' he declared forcibly, 'I know you, and you know me, and in my book that's good enough. I'm willing to put up a show, if that's what you want, but don't expect me to turn into a movie Romeo overnight,' he added with a grin. 'Besides,' he tacked on maddeningly, 'you're no sultry heroine yourself. Look at those faded jeans of yours. Haven't you anything more feminine to wear?' he demanded. 'If I'm going to play the part of the lover, you might give me some encouragement,' he complained lightly, but there was an imp of amusement lurking behind his blue eyes.

There he goes again! Vicky thought furiously.
Making fun of me. 'I don't want you to play act,'
she ground out between clenched teeth. 'I just want
you to realise that it's no go. I'm not going to
change my mind, I'm going to Albury to get a job,
and that's final!'

'You're doing no such thing!' Ross said forcibly.
'So you can forget it. What the devil could you do
anyway? Apart from waiting at tables—or standing
behind the counter of a multiple store. If you think
I'm letting you do that, then you've another think
coming. Here's where you belong, and where
you're staying.'

Vicky recognised that tone of voice; it meant no
arguing. The master had spoken! She took a deep
breath. She knew she was asking for trouble, but
this was one fight that Ross wasn't going to win.
'Says who?' she spat out furiously, jumping out of
her chair and standing glaring up at him with her
hands on her slender hips and her chin thrust out
in defiance.

'You know the answer to that one,' said Ross in
his quiet determined voice. 'Go by all means. I
can't keep an hourly check on you, but I'm warning
you, I'll drag you back each time you make the
break. You'll see it my way eventually,' he added
smoothly.

'Why?' said Vicky, her curiosity overcoming her
fury. 'Why should you bother?' Her smooth brow
creased in a frown and then her brows went up.
'Pride, is it?' she asked silkily. 'Because everyone
will think you've turned me down? They'll never

dream it was the other way round, will they?' she added furiously.

Ross's dark brows lifted at this. 'Think I care two hoots for gossip?' he said dryly. 'You ought to know better than that. No, I guess I feel responsible for you,' he added quietly, supplying fuel to the fire already raging in Vicky.

'I'm over nineteen,' she said with as much dignity as she could muster, although she wanted to scream it out at him. He had made her feel an encumbrance. As he saw it he was only doing his duty, the big brother act again, she thought bitterly. 'I'm over the age of consent,' she told him coldly, 'and I can even vote,' she added sarcastically.

Ross nodded grimly. 'In your case, age has nothing to do with it. You've a long way to go before you grow up. Perhaps you're right about not marrying me—not for a year or so anyway. I'd say even more than that,' his narrowed gaze swept over her slight figure. 'I guess that's partly the reason why I haven't pushed things before, but we've plenty of time,' he said comfortably. 'Look, if you're so all-fired set on a change, I'll arrange for you to visit my aunt in Sydney for a spell. How about that?' he suggested quietly.

Vicky's eyes went to the carpet on the floor. She was tempted to accept the offer. It would get her away from the station and give her time to think. She took a deep breath. She didn't need time to think. She knew what she wanted, and that was her freedom from the contract that Ross was determined to honour. At this point a vision of

Mrs Janson arose in her mind, and of the way she had tried to groom Vicky into the kind of wife she wanted for her son. She knew the aunt he spoke of was her sister, and recalled meeting her a few years back—a very smart woman, who moved in the exclusive circles of Sydney's rich, and who would no doubt look upon Vicky as a country cousin, and worse still, take on the unfinished task of grooming her for her future role as Ross's wife.

She would have no freedom. Her friends and acquaintances would be chosen for her, and she would be known as 'Ross's girl' wherever she went. A wave of bitterness swept over her. 'No, thank you,' she said quietly, concealing her hurt, for she was sure Ross's intention was the same as his mother's had been. A little grooming would be necessary to bring her up to scratch. He was stuck with her and was trying to make the best of a bad deal. His earlier hints on her clothes had proved that.

Ross, seeing her hesitation, mistook the reason. 'Well, think about it,' he said quietly, 'and forget the other,' he ordered, back to his old authoritative tone.

Vicky's eyes left the carpet and met his blue gaze. 'I'm sorry, I can't do that,' she said with quiet dignity, and there was something in her bearing that did more to convince Ross of her determination than any of her earlier statements.

'Can't, or won't?' he said softly, through narrowed eyes. 'Not even to please me? Even though I got your father out of one hell of a tight hole?' he said harshly.

Vicky's eyes widened as she stared back at him. This was not the Ross she knew. This was a subtle kind of blackmail, and the last ruse she would have expected him to use. She knew he liked his own way, but to go that far—She swallowed. 'That's below the belt,' she said quietly, her blazing eyes showing her feelings.

'When the devil drives,' said Ross, but the answering blaze in his eyes told her he was as angry as she was.

'And what devil's driving you?' Vicky replied furiously, 'Pride—that's what it is, isn't it? You're only thinking how bad it will look for you if I move out, aren't you? All right!' she ground out. 'I'll stay—but only because you've made me feel beholden to you. No doubt I shall have to marry you for the same reason,' she added bitterly. 'I presume you paid a high price for the station. High enough to include the extras,' she spat out at him. She knew that she was being ungrateful, and that her words were cruel, but she was goaded beyond reason. It wasn't her fault that her father had made a fool of himself, but she was being made to pay the price of his folly.

Ross took a step nearer to her, and she knew by the blaze in his eyes that he was having trouble keeping his hands off her. 'As a matter of fact,' he blazed out at her, 'I paid twice what it was worth.' His jaw tightened as he looked beyond her at a spot on the sitting-room wall. 'Your father's been living on capital for years. I warned him again and again that he couldn't go on taking it out, and not putting it back, but I guess it was easier the other way,' he added harshly. 'The station's a shadow of its former state. It was prosperous enough when your father took it over. I guess it's not entirely his fault. He's no business sense. You either have it or you don't—and he hadn't. If he'd listened to me all those years ago and put a manager in, then it wouldn't have taken long to repair the damage; as it is, there's a hell of a lot to see to and it's going to take twice as long to lick into shape. That's why I put Jake in charge. It wouldn't have worked the other way. Jake's a good man and should have been put in charge ages ago. He's the one who's really been running the station.'

Vicky couldn't meet his eyes. She felt ashamed of herself. Jake couldn't have kept things going without some help himself, someone to put him on the right lines, and she knew who that someone had been. She wished that she had known how it had been, but it was too late now. This was something that Ross had never meant to tell her. He was not a man to betray such confidences, particularly when it concerned her father. It just went to show how far she had goaded him, she thought miserably. Still keeping her eyes on the carpet, she said in a low voice, 'I'm sorry, Ross, I didn't know how things were.'

It was meant to be an apology, but it did not have the desired effect, it only seemed to make Ross even more furious. 'No,' he bit out harshly, 'there's not much you know about anything, is

there? That's why I'm holding you to your word
about staying put. I've too much on my plate to
hare off after you. There's too many drifters
around on the lookout for little green girls like you.
As for having to marry me,' he gave a twisted sneer,
'I shouldn't worry too much about that. I want a
helpmate, not a wife who's liable to kick over the
traces through boredom, so you can safely forget
that part of it,' he added meaningly.

Stunned, Vicky looked up just in time to see
Ross's tall frame striding out of the door, the door
almost slamming after him.

The odd catch phrase of 'was it something I
said?' floated through her mind, and she gave an
hysterical giggle, then closed her eyes as she fought
for calmness. She'd got what she wanted, hadn't
she? Ross wouldn't marry her if she was the last
girl in the country. She had known that he didn't
love her, but she had been totally unprepared to
hear what he really thought of her. There was
nothing, she thought with tears in her eyes, to
compare with a showdown. At least she now knew
where she stood with him. As far as he was concerned she was a confounded nuisance to him. It
oughtn't to have come as such a shock to her. She
had known it all the time, but to actually hear him
say so—She wiped the tears from her eyes, then
straightened her slim shoulders. Tomorrow she'd
feel better about things. When Ross did eventually
marry, she could carry out her delayed plans for
her future. Whoever was his bride-to-be, and Vicky
didn't envy her one little bit, would make certain

that his attention stayed on her, and not on Vicky Dale, and giving Vicky freedom at last from any obligation Ross felt towards her.

CHAPTER FOUR

The following day Jake and Mary moved into the homestead. Their personal furniture had been packed away in one of the storehouses awaiting their final move into the quarters Ross was having built for them.

For her part Vicky was glad of the company. Mary's quiet and soothing manner, and natural acceptance of any situation that arose, would help her to get her own troubles back into perspective again.

For someone who had gained an important victory over Ross—an almost unprecedented happening—she was curiously deflated. It had been a long time before she had got to sleep the previous night. It was not so much Ross's condemnation of her as a young and foolish girl whom he felt responsible for, but the altered status in their relationship. Whatever else she had thought of Ross, she had considered him a friend, even when she was furious with him; her fury soon abated as it did with fights between families, all being forgiven because of strong ties of affection.

They ought, she had argued silently with herself,

have been able to talk things over in a reasonable way. It was not like Ross to lose his temper like that, but she had never stood up to him before, had never had reason to. Since he had taken over Jarra Station, his visits to Dale's Creek and the Dales visits to his home, had been few and far between. They were in constant touch through the normal running of the stations, but that was a business contact and not a social one.

Had they both changed so much? she thought bewilderedly. They were strangers now, and it was none of her doing. It had been his choice to spend all his time on the station. In the early days, shortly after he had taken over the station, there had been local events, that they would normally have attended together, but he had put duty before pleasure. At the time, this was understandable, but as the weeks and months passed, it became a habit.

Looking back now with hindsight, Vicky could see how much of a tedious duty those outings must have been for him, escorting a wide-eyed teenager, as she had been in those days, to various organised amusements.

It had never occurred to Vicky that Ross might have been bored, or that given the chance he would have passed this task on to someone else. She had taken his company for granted, and had never known what it felt like to have to rely on others for company. It was small wonder that she had no friends of her own age. She had acquaintances, of course, girls she had gone to school with, and that

she met at the get-togethers during the years, Cassy
Brook and her friend Lucy Sean being two of them,
but acquaintances were all they were, and after
overhearing Cassy's remarks regarding herself,
Vicky was not likely to seek a closer friendship with
either of them.

Her thoughts were still on her encounter with
Ross when she had awoken that morning, and recalling his remarks upon her clothing, she was
tempted to put on a skirt. She had not worn a skirt
for ages, she thought, and stared at her old faded
jeans, then gave a shrug. If she did dress up, Ross
would be sure it was for his benefit. She scowled.
It wasn't worth it. Besides, she felt more comfortable in her old jeans and she was not out to impress
anyone, least of all Ross!

After her shower, however, and recalling that
Jake and Mary would be moving in that morning,
she compromised by wearing her second-best trews
and a crisp white blouse. She ought to put on some
sort of a show for Mary's sake, she told herself, as
she went down to prepare the breakfast. Mary was
always neatly dressed.

Her father's query of 'was she going somewhere?'
did not make for a good start to the day, and only
proved Ross's point that she took no trouble over
her appearance, and she gave a dignified reply to
the effect that as Mary and Jake were coming that
morning, she had decided to make an effort, and
she did not miss her father's swift look of relief at
this reply.

It was then that she realised that he did not know

the result of her talk with Ross the previous evening, as she had gone to bed by the time he had come back from Jake's.

Not only Ross's pride would have been hurt if she had gone ahead with her plan to find herself a job, she thought ruefully. She had forgotten to take her father's feelings into account. There would most certainly be talk. She sighed inwardly. It had seemed such a good idea at the time, too.

She was reminded of Ross's bald comments when he had accused her of only thinking of herself. Not that he had actually said that, but she was sure that that was what he had in mind when he said that she hadn't grown up. She took a deep breath. 'About getting a job,' she began slowly, 'I suppose there's plenty of time. I promised Ross I wouldn't do anything about it for a while,' she tacked on lamely, and seeing her father's relieved smile, added, 'It's something I'll keep in mind, though.'

'Sure, sure,' agreed her father hastily, as he handed her his cup for a refill. 'I guess things will look up now that Mary's around to keep you company.' He stared down at the kitchen table. 'You know, I'm looking forward to taking a back seat,' he commented thoughtfully. 'Didn't like the idea at first, mind you, but Ross was right to put Jake in charge,' he grinned at Vicky. 'Seems he's been coaching him for a manager's job for some time. It will take a lot of worry off my shoulders, too. Things aren't the same as they were in your grandfather's day. It's one damn form after another now—all paper work.'

Vicky's brows lifted as she handed him his second cup of coffee. 'Forms you'll still have to fill in. You're doing the paper work, aren't you?' she commented dryly.

'I only fill in what I'm told to fill in,' he replied airily. 'Things are changing around here now that it's under new management. That's Ross's headache now and he's welcome to it,' he added with a certain amount of relish in his voice.

As Vicky sat sipping her coffee, her thoughts returned yet again to Ross's comments the previous evening on her father's lack of ability to run the station profitably, but they couldn't all be clever, she thought tartly. Not everyone had Ross Janson's genius in making things work, and very few would come up to his high standards, but he wouldn't see things that way. He didn't rate her father very high, and rated his daughter even lower! she thought ironically.

Jake and Mary arrived shortly after breakfast, Mary, as always, looking trim in a plain green sleeveless dress. Her brown wavy hair that seemed to spring away from her forehead now showed a light sprinkling of grey, but her round pleasant features and deep brown eyes never seemed to alter. Her expression was continually one of placidity, although Vicky detected a trace of anxiety in her eyes as they met hers. Jake had obviously told her of Vicky's first reaction to the news that he was taking over as manager, and it was plain that Mary was not too happy about it herself, but Vicky's cheery welcome and amused quip that her father was looking forward to a change of cook quickly reassured her, and they chatted together amicably while Mary helped Vicky with the breakfast dishes. Mary insisted on doing the washing of the dishes, and leaving Vicky to dry.

When this was done, and Vicky was putting the plates away, Mary, wiping her hands on the towel, commented lightly, 'Anything else you want done? I've only to unpack our cases, and that won't take long, so you can go ahead with what you've planned.'

Vicky closed the door of the cupboard and turned to look at her. 'I've nothing planned,' she said in a surprised voice. 'Only a sweater I'm hoping to finish in time for the cold spell,' she added with a grin.

Mary's eyes rested on Vicky's second best trews and on to her white blouse. 'Oh, I thought——' she said quickly, then seeing Vicky scowl, subsided into silence.

'First Dad and then you,' Vicky said crossly. 'Everything else is in the wash,' she added defiantly.

'Ross came over last night, didn't he?' Mary murmured slyly.

Vicky glared at her. 'And what's that got to do with it?' she demanded.

Mary's eyes crinkled at the corners. 'Nothing—nothing at all,' she said with a hint of amusement in her voice.

'Well, for once you're right!' Vicky said tartly, and practically throwing the small wisp of an apron that Mary had handed her into the dresser drawer, she marched out of the kitchen and straight up to her room, where she immediately changed out of her trews and back into her jeans. She also discarded the blouse and got herself an old T-shirt to wear. 'It comes to something,' she muttered darkly to herself, 'when I can't wear anything decent without folks thinking I'm trying to please Ross Janson!'

The sooner Mary knew the truth the better, she thought. In fact, the sooner everyone knew the better. Not that that would stop people thinking the same way as Mary did. Whatever she tried to do that in any way differed from her normal routine, it would be put down as a calculated effort on her behalf to attract Ross's attention. It would simply not occur to them that the break had come from her and not from him, and she was going to have to steel herself to receive a lot of sympathy from outsiders. Not that that would worry her, she thought furiously, as she started to make her bed, but she did wish that others would see things from her point of view for once.

Mary's swift, hastily concealed grin when Vicky reappeared a short while later, did nothing to soothe Vicky's ruffled feelings, and she wished that she had been able to go ahead with her plan to leave the station, even if only to please herself what she did, not only in the matter of dress.

Her annoyance soon passed, however. It was

impossible to remain cross with Mary for long, for it was not her fault that things had gone wrong for Vicky, and it was important to her to make Mary see things from her point of view.

With Jake ensconced in the study with her father, and Mary fully occupied in checking up on the larder supplies, and tut-tutting on the low state of the freezer items, Vicky found herself at a loose end.

Normally this would not have worried her; she had always managed to fill in her time before. There was always the housework to do, and the washing and ironing, but she never had a set pattern to her day. If she felt like leaving everything and going down to the creek for a swim, she did just that, or if she wanted to go into town when her hair wanted cutting and shaping, she just got into her old Holden and off she went, but these trips were few and far between, and she had a good reason at the present time to stay clear of the town. There were too many gossips there who would be burning to know why her father had semi-retired, for that was the story that would be put around, not that Ross had taken over.

That the news would rate a headline in the gossip column of the local grapevine, Vicky was certain. She was also certain that the open lines had been working overtime since that morning. Jake and Mary's sudden move out of the married quarters into the homestead must have caused a lot of speculation, and Vicky was sure she would find herself

having to answer various questions as to the state of
her father's health, and she would have to carefully
work out the answers, something on the lines of
her father needing a rest from the responsibilities
of running a station, and at the same time make it
clear that he was not ill, just tired.

This sort of enquiry she felt she could deal with
adequately, but she was not so sure about the personal angle and how to tackle the innocent-sound-
ing enquiries regarding Ross and herself, or the
downright inquisitive inquisition she would receive
from certain people, if she were unlucky enough to
encounter them, on whether a date had been fixed
for the wedding.

To state categorically that there would be no
wedding would cause an even bigger headline for
the gossips to chew over than her father's semi-
retirement. The more Vicky thought about this, the
more she could see her father's and Ross's point of
view. It would look bad for Ross, and without the
whole mess coming out as to how Ross had
obtained the station, Vicky could see no way out.
Not unless they hired a town crier to give out a
statement announcing their broken engagement,
and that it was a joint decision on both their parts,
she thought dismally.

Vicky's wish to avoid a town visit was doomed
to failure, because Mary had other plans, and
before she could decide what she was going to do
that morning, Mary asked her if she would mind
running her into town to collect some supplies. 'We
might as well make a morning of it,' she said with

a smile. 'I haven't had coffee and cream cakes at Ma Harper's for months.'

Under the circumstances there was nothing Vicky could do about it. There was no one else Mary could ask. She didn't drive herself, and Vicky could not get out of the trip by offering her the loan of her car. Quite apart from that, it would have been a snub to Mary, who obviously thought she would enjoy a morning out.

On the ride to town, Vicky was very tempted to confide in Mary. With her on her side she felt she would have a staunch ally in spiking the rumours that were bound to be around, but she was not sure how much Mary knew of her father's affairs, and although Jake either knew or had worked it out for himself, it didn't mean that Mary knew too.

Mary's tentative comments just before they reached the town gave Vicky the lead she wanted. 'Your father's taken it well, Vicky,' she said quietly, being careful to keep her gaze on the passing landscape.

Vicky cast her a quick look before she turned her attention back to the road again. 'If you ask me, he's relieved,' she said. 'He's actually looking forward to taking a back seat.' Then on an impulse, she asked quickly, 'How much do you know, Mary?'

Mary looked at her. 'You mean what do we tell the noseys?' she asked with a smile in her voice. 'We maintain a united front, that's what,' she added. 'Your father's decided he wants a rest and has given the reins to Ross. He'd have it anyway, later, wouldn't he?' she said complacently.

'Not necessarily,' Vicky replied in a low voice. 'You see, I'm not going to marry him.'

She felt rather than saw Mary's swift surprised glance at her. 'Since when?' Mary demanded.

Vicky gave a shrug of her slim shoulders. 'Does it matter?' she asked. 'I'd decided not to go through with it before—well, before Dad—you know what I mean.'

'And what does Ross say about that?' asked Mary quietly. 'Or doesn't he know yet?' she asked sardonically.

Vicky managed to control the spurt of temper she always felt when Ross's authority was mentioned. Why did no one think of her? 'Of course he knows,' she bit out, 'and he agrees with me,' she hesitated, 'but I guess it's kind of awkward for him right now, but I wasn't to know——' she broke off lamely, then added defiantly, 'anyhow, that's how things are.'

'Vicky Dale, you want your head examined!' Mary said indignantly. 'Why, Ross is the nicest man—and the most eligible—for miles around! Do you realise what it's going to look like for him? Awkward isn't the word! Look, have you thought this out?' she asked quietly. 'Ross will be made to look the biggest heel this side of Canberra! For goodness' sake don't broadcast it around—not yet anyway, not until things have settled down. Whatever's got into you will have worked itself out by then, you'll see,' she added soothingly.

'I do see,' Vicky said crossly, 'and of course I'll not say anything. It's up to Ross to work something out, but I'm not much good at telling lies, and I hate it when I'm teased about the wedding. If it's awkward for Ross, it's twice as bad for me—but then nobody thinks of that,' she ended bitterly, as they entered the outer precincts of the town.

Mary laid a light hand on Vicky's arm. 'They do think of you, Vicky,' she said quietly, 'that's why it's going to be worse for Ross, but don't worry about it. I'm sure it will work itself out,' she added, as the car drew to a stop in a parking lot outside the large main store that Mary wanted to visit.

It was all very well being told not to worry, Vicky thought sardonically, as she got out of the car and handed Mary the shopping carrier, but it was her future, not Mary's, and she only hoped that Ross would keep to his threat of not marrying her, for it looked as if that was her only hope, but he had been good and mad when he had said that, she thought, and would probably change his mind when he had calmed down.

All she had to do was to keep him riled, she thought dryly, as she accompanied Mary into the store, and stopped in her tracks as it suddenly occurred to her that she had the answer, and it was son simple! She would have a golden opportunity to show everyone that they were just not suited, because she was certain Ross would give the shearing gang a 'shindig' as he had put it, and what better chance would she have?

Mary tugged at her sleeve. 'Come on, or we won't have time for coffee,' she said, breaking into Vicky's happy musings.

Vicky followed Mary's back round the store, but her mind was busy with plans. She would do something at that party that would infuriate Ross—she didn't know what, but no doubt she would come up with something. She had to, she was not likely to get another chance for ages. A row in public would be just the job, she thought happily, and if only she had a ring that she could throw disdainfully at his feet, she thought wistfully, it would finalise the whole thing.

With all the immediate provisions packed away in the Holden's boot, and the rest of the freezer goods to come by van, Mary and Vicky headed for Ma Harper's and a cup of creamy coffee and equally creamy cakes.

As Vicky had feared, there were several of the town gossips already cosily ensconced behind the small tables indulging in their favourite hobby of discussing local titbits of news, and Vicky's new-found lift of spirits suffered a relapse as greetings were called to them as they threaded their way to a table by the window.

'How's your father, Vicky?' was the opening gambit put forward by Mrs Campton, a buxom woman with a sharp nose for gossip, and the local undertaker's wife, and Vicky wondered caustically if she was looking for trade for her husband, and shot a quick glance towards Mary that plainly said,

'Here we go!' before answering lightly, 'Very well, thank you, Mrs Campton. How's Mr Campton? she countermanded.

'Thriving,' boomed Mrs Campton, obviously disappointed with the result of her opening skirmish on the gossip front, and turned her attention to Mary. 'I hear Jake's to be congratulated, Mary—guess you'll soon be owning your own station,' she added playfully.

Mary's brows went up at this. 'No chance of that,' she replied steadily, and Vicky knew that she was furious with Mrs Campton but was too wise to show it. It had been a stupid question and a thoughtless one. Every foreman or manager dreamed of owning a station one day, but at the present day cost of land, dreams were all they were and all they were likely to be. It was then that Vicky remembered that Mrs Campton's brother had lost out on the foreman's job that had become vacant on Jake's promotion, and that she was probably attempting to rile Mary, who wasn't having any of it.

Mrs Sayer, who owned a boutique a few doors down the road from the café, then joined in the discussion, deciding to give her friend Mrs Campton a hand in the fishing expedition. 'And what will your father find to do with his time?' she asked Vicky, assuming an innocent expression but her eyes behind her hornrimmed spectacles giving the lie to her casual question.

'Take a well-earned rest,' Vicky said bitingly, trying to keep her annoyance out of her voice, and thinking that if she did take a job in town this was one area she would have to keep clear of.

Mary, sensing trouble, came to Vicky's rescue, with a smooth, 'It will be several years before Mr Dale actually retires, and a good deal more before he needs Mr Campton's services,' she added dryly, turning to the waitress who had just appeared and ordering coffee and cakes for two, effectively putting an end to any further discussion on that topic.

The next topic, however, was not so easily disposed of, for Mrs Sayer, with an eye to the future, turned to Vicky just before she and her friend left the café. 'I've a nice selection of wedding dresses in, Vicky,' she murmured hopefully.

In the act of swallowing a sip of her coffee, Vicky almost choked, and Mary, unable to suppress a grin, again came to her rescue with, 'It's early days for that, too,' and greeted a woman who had just entered the café and stood behind Mrs Sayer and Mrs Campton, 'Oh, hallo, Mrs Brook, how's that back of yours?' leaving them to make their exit without any satisfaction, although Mrs Campton's mutterings about certain folk taking a lot on themselves was not lost on Mary and Vicky.

'You see how it is?' Vicky said indignantly as they left the café a short while later. 'Thank goodness it's not market day, and we only met two of them!' she added with heartfelt gratitude.

'It's the same for Ross, remember?' Mary said quietly, as Vicky unlocked the car and opened the passenger door for her.

'Ross can take care of himself,' Vicky commented darkly, and then gave a sigh of resignation as she got into the car. 'It's difficult, though, isn't it?' she said despondently.

Mary wriggled herself into a more comfortable position on the sagging seat of the old car, and looked at Vicky. 'I should leave it to Ross,' she said comfortably. 'He'll know how to handle it. The trouble with you two is that you don't really know each other,' she added thoughtfully.

Vicky gave her a surprised look before she turned on the ignition. 'Know each other too well, you mean, don't you?' she queried ironically.

Mary shook her head. 'You think about it,' she said quietly. 'You haven't seen a great deal of each other for some time, have you?' she asked. 'Not since he took over his father's station, I mean, and there's hardly been time——' she hesitated, and Vicky knew what was coming next. 'Well, what I'm trying to say is that he hasn't courted you, has he?' Mary eventually got out, casting a sidelong look at Vicky.

Vicky felt the colour coming to her cheeks but kept her eyes on the road. 'Can you see Ross casting sheep's eyes at me, or at anyone else for that matter?' she asked pithily. 'He might make the occasional grab at his beloved,' she added, still keeping her eyes firmly fixed ahead of her, 'but who wants that?' she demanded.

Mary gave a deep chuckle. 'You'd be surprised,' she said teasingly, 'how many there'd be in that queue.'

Vicky negotiated a sharp bend before she answered, 'But that's just it!' she exclaimed crossly. 'I don't happen to be one of them.' After a moment's silence, she added slowly, 'You know, you were right when you said that we didn't really know each other. I—well, we—had a row last night,' she took a deep breath. 'I guess I heard a few home truths about the way he really feels about me.' She gave Mary a quick look before she turned her attention back to the road again. 'He sees me as a spoilt madam who doesn't know what's good for her. Oh, not only over my wanting to back out of the marriage, but over the question of my getting a job,' and as she sensed Mary's surprise over this piece of news, she added quickly, 'I'd made up my mind to get out and start earning my own living before Ross took over the station, so it's nothing to do with that, but I can't get anyone to believe me,' she tacked on bitterly. 'Dad and Ross put it down to loneliness, and that I was a bit low. I was low all right,' she added emphatically. 'I was fed up with everything, and needed a change, but all they can see is how bad it will look for them if I go ahead!'

Mary looked at her. 'What brought all that on?' she asked quietly.

Vicky's brows lifted, as she changed gear. 'What brought what on?' she asked puzzledly.

'All this business about leaving Dale's Creek,' Mary said. 'You never cared for town life before, and you couldn't have changed overnight, not unless something happened. What was it?'

Vicky cast her an exasperated look. 'You're just like them,' she said crossly. 'Why should I have a reason for wanting a change?'

'Because you're you,' Mary replied calmly. 'I've watched you grow up, remember? I recall the times that your mother had to coax you to put on a party dress and go to those parties, and goodness knows how many excuses you'd put forward for not attending. So come on—what happened?' she asked again.

Seeing no help for it but to tell the truth, Vicky told Mary what she had overheard Cassy and Lucy say about her in the hairdressers that day, ending with, 'It made me think, you see. I'm grateful to them. I hadn't really thought about the future before—it always seemed a long way away. The thing is,' she explained carefully, 'that they were perfectly right. Why should Ross have to marry me? He doesn't love me any more than I love him. It's not as if I were a beauty, is it? I tell you, they feel sorry for him, and if he wasn't so autocratic and so set on getting his own way, I'd feel sorry for him too. As it is, I feel sorrier for myself. It would be better if I did love him, believe me,' she added furiously, 'then I'd go down the altar like a lamb, and everybody would be happy——' She stopped abruptly, and hot tears scalded her lids, but she blinked them irritably away and concentrated on her driving.

Mary did not actually say, 'There, there,' but her tone implied it. 'I can see you have a problem,' she said quietly. 'I guess we'll have to work on it.

You know, I used to wonder if Ross had a thing
about Ella Waden,' and at Vicky's quick look at
her, nodded slowly, 'Oh, that was years ago. He'd
be about eighteen then,' she went on slowly. 'You'd
be about twelve. Ella's round about twenty-four
now, isn't she?' she queried casually, 'and she's
never married has she?' she hinted, still with that
casual note in her voice.

Vicky saw the homestead boundary fence in
front of them and gave a curt nod of her head. 'So
you think——?' she left the sentence unfinished.

Mary nodded her head. 'Well, it would solve
things from your point of view, wouldn't it?' she
said. 'We'll have to get our heads together on it,
won't we?' she suggested smilingly.

Vicky drove on steadily, and gave another curt
nod but said nothing. For some reason the suggestion did not appeal to her. Ross ought to do his
own courting, she thought angrily—if he could
spare the time, that was! But it might be interesting
at that, she thought with a sudden lift of spirits,
and flung Mary a grateful look. It was nice to have
someone on your side, she thought, particularly if
it happened to be someone like Mary.

CHAPTER FIVE

Two days later the news that Ross was giving the shearers a send-off in the form of free beer and eats at Jarra Station the next evening, when they were due to finish at Dale's Creek, filtered over the grapevine.

Vicky felt a little peeved that it was not being held at Dale's Creek, since it outlined the fact that the two stations were now amalgamated, and that Jarra was the main station, and when Mrs George rang later that morning asking for Mary's help in preparing the mountain of food that would have to be got ready, and requesting that Mary make some meat patties, Vicky felt the altered status in the station even more keenly.

Ross would have told Mrs George to get Mary to help out, and it was a wonder to Vicky that he hadn't ordered her presence too, but then he wouldn't have thought that she could contribute any useful help in that line. She would be expected to attend, of course, but only in the role of a guest.

Nevertheless, Vicky did give Mary a hand by carrying out such mundane tasks as clearing up, and washing the mixture bowls, ready for the next batch of patties to be made.

The rest of that day passed pleasantly, and although Vicky would never have admitted it, she

had loved the bustle and the general air of expectancy that hung over the homestead. It was like
the old times. Parties were few and far between
these days, and although it was strictly a station
affair, there were sure to be some invitations
thrown out to their nearest neighbours and that
were bound to be accepted.

Had things gone according to plan, Vicky was
sure that Ross would have used the occasion to
announce their wedding date, and the fact that no
such an announcement would be made would cause
a few eyebrows to be raised, but no doubt Ross
would handle that side of things with his usual
aplomb, she thought dryly.

The following afternoon, Vicky ran Mary up to
Jarra to help Mrs George with the cutting of the
sandwiches. She had always been in a little awe of
the stout, rather formidable-looking housekeeper
who had been with the Janson family since Ross
was in his early teens. What she had thought of
Vicky as the new mistress of Jarra, Vicky could
not hazard a guess, but as the situation would not
now arise, it was of no consequence.

Whenever Vicky visited Jarra, she was never at
her ease. It stemmed from a sense of inequality on
her part, and this was outlined by the imposing
homestead set in well-tended gardens, and her
inward inability to come up to the standards Ross's
mother had tried to instil into her.

Dale's Creek, in comparison to Jarra, would
come a poor second in the grandeur stakes, if it
qualified at all. It was a homestead for working

people whose interests lay beyond the old brick and
wood building, and had no other pretensions. It
was simply a homestead. There were no lawned
areas and well kept flower borders as around Jarra,
which looked to Vicky's rather sceptical eyes as if
it had been bodily lifted out of one of Canberra's
more fashionable housing areas and dumped right
in the middle of surrounding pasture land.

It had not always been like that. Vicky's mother
had often spoken of the old days before the homestead had been renovated. In those days Jarra and
Dale's Creek had been much on a par, and Dale's
Creek was considered a more superior dwelling
owing to its size rather than its elegance.

When old Dan Janson had died, and his son
John took over the reins, his new bride took over
the renovation of the homestead. Money being no
problem, she set out to produce a dwelling that she
could live in, and Vicky's musings on the subject
had not been all that far out. The homestead would
not have looked out of place in any of the richer
suburbs of a city, and all it lacked was a swimming
pool, according to Vicky's amused thoughts on the
matter.

As Vicky stood next to Mary in the large modern
kitchen of Jarra, she was reminded of her mother's
comments on the renovations, saying somewhat
wistfully, 'Why, four could work in that kitchen
and still not get in each other's way!'

Mary's low remark on the side to Vicky as they
waited for Mrs George's appearance, that she
would need a pilot's licence to operate the cooker,

echoed Vicky's thoughts on the matter, and she gave her a conspiratorial grin, but she could have hugged her. Mary was a 'Dale's Creeker' through and through, and no ostentatious equipment was likely to woo her to the other side, for that was how Vicky saw things, and how she must have felt for a long time, without realising it.

By five o'clock, all was prepared for the party, which would start around seven-thirty. It was held in the store barn at the back of the homestead, and the long low bench was left in its usual position at the end of the roomy barn and was now loaded with piles of sandwiches, meat patties and various cold meats, all covered with damp cloths to keep fresh.

The store's serving counter had been brought into action as a bar at the side of the food bench, and a huge urn of tea placed sedately on a shelf behind the counter for those who preferred a milder beverage.

Mary had been roped in to help with the serving of the food, and after much argument Vicky had allied herself with Mary, taking on the tea counter, although neither Mary nor Mrs George had approved of this arrangement. It was Vicky's task to entertain the guests—not serve them, though neither of them actually said so, this was clearly what they thought, but Vicky was having none of it. As Mary had said, parties were not Vicky's favourite events, and as long as she felt useful, she was happy.

They were back at Dale's Creek in good time to

prepare themselves a light meal to keep them going until the evening, and to change into what Mary referred to as their 'glad rags'.

Mary's ideas, however, slightly differed from Vicky's, for she frowned at Vicky's choice of trews and blouse. 'Haven't you a nice dress, Vicky?' she asked, as she straightened Jake's tie in a wifely way while they waited for Gordon Dale to join them.

Her choice of words was unfortunate, for it echoed Ross's sentiments, and Vicky swallowed back the cutting remark that she would please herself how she dressed. 'I'm more comfortable like this,' she said, surprising herself, for her tone was very mild.

'You'll be the only one in trews,'Mary persisted. 'You know how it is. We don't often get a chance to dress up. All the frills and furbelows will be out, you'll see,' she added.

Jake coughed. 'I'll see what's holding Gordon up,' he said hastily, sensing a battle royal between the women, and coward-like made his retreat.

Vicky's lips firmed as she looked back at Mary. 'You've not gone to town,' she said accusingly, casting her eye over Mary's simple dark blue dress, 'so why should I?' she asked.

Mary's brows lifted. 'I'm a working girl,' she said with a grin, showing that she had not taken exception to Vicky's remark but had taken it as Vicky had meant her to take it.

'So am I,' Vicky replied quickly.

'You know what I mean,' Mary answered, and

gave a sigh of exasperation. 'Do wear a dress, Vicky, please. You'll feel quite out of it if you don't,' she pleaded.

As much as she wanted to argue the point, Vicky suddenly gave in. Having Mary there brought back memories of her mother and how she used to coax her into dressing up for a party, and she reluctantly went back to her room to comply with Mary's request.

Back in her room, Vicky wished she had not given in to Mary. To make a special effort now would be sure to give Ross ideas, and she liked things as they were. He would reason that woman-like she had taken heed of his remarks on her manner of dress, and taken trouble to please him. Before she knew what was going on, he would be announcing their wedding date, she thought irritably.

When she reappeared ten minutes later, wearing a soft pink dress with a flounced skirt, she earned an approving nod from Mary, and a quick grin from Jake, but her father's look of surprise and whimsical remark that he had a lovely daughter brought a lump to her throat. Her mother had used the same tactic years ago to make Vicky feel good when she had complied with her wishes, and it made Vicky feel worse, rather than better.

For a moment or so it was touch and go whether she went to the party or not. She didn't want to go one little bit, and only the thought of carrying out her cherished plan of goading Ross into having a blazing row in public with her made her allow herself to be ushered into her father's Land Rover along with Mary and Jake.

By nine o'clock the party was in full swing, and Vicky, enveloped in one of Mrs George's aprons to protect her dress from any accident that might occur from the tea counter, felt safe from any persuasion to join in the dancing that started up when one of the station hands produced a violin, and was soon joined by another with a mouth organ. After a short time, another station hand appeared with a huge old accordion, and when some enterprising hand put a dilapidated-looking saucepan to use as a makeshift drum the evening was set for success as an improvised barn dance.

Looking round at the happy assembly, Vicky had to concede that Mary had been right. She would have felt very much out of it if she had stuck to her guns and worn her trews.

Even Mrs George had made a concession in the matter of dress, and had discarded the dark dresses that Vicky could only recall ever seeing her wear for a light summery one, and actually took part in the dancing at Ross's instigation.

Up until the dancing started, Vicky had not seen much of Ross; he had been busy seeing that the shearing gang were liberally served with refreshments, and chatting to the other landowners. When he had glanced over her way, Vicky had still been covered by Mrs George's apron that was so large that it gave no clue to the dress beneath, and she thought she detected a look of exasperation from him before he turned his attention back to his guests.

The look pleased her. It made a good start to the evening, and come what may, she meant to hang on to the apron, thus annoying him further.

When the dancing started, however, her plans went awry, for it was Ross who demanded that she come out from behind the counter and join in the fun, and no amount of black looks or excuses that she was quite happy where she was would he accept, and his annoyed, 'Are you coming? Or do I fetch you?' produced a shout of laughter from his men, and murmurings of, 'That's it, Ross. You start as you mean to go on,' from the delighted bystanders, giving Vicky no choice but to comply with his wishes, for it was no mean threat on Ross's part, and however much she wanted to annoy him, she wanted it on her terms, not on his.

His amused, 'And you can take that tent off,' as she stamped round the counter towards him further infuriated her, and did nothing for Mrs George's aplomb, who after a surprised blink gave a smile of amusement. No one else but Ross would have got away with such a remark, Vicky thought furiously, as she flung the apron off and turned to face Ross.

For a fleeting second his bright blue gaze flicked over her slight figure in her pink dress, then he gave a lift of the eyebrows and then gave a jerk of his autocratic head at the musicians to start playing, as he led her on to the floor. 'You'll do,' he said grandly, as he whirled her into the dance.

Do for what? wondered Vicky crossly, although

she already knew the answer. She would do for him, was what he was saying, and she hoped that no one else had heard those words, for it would hardly help her in her campaign. He had decided to forgive her, she thought sourly, and intended to keep up the pretence of their arranged engagement.

As Ross twirled her round in the dance with twice as much energy than was necessary, making Vicky feel like a bullfighter's cloak, a sense of desperation crept over her. If Ross was determined to go ahead, what chance did she have? What chance did either of them have for true happiness? She would always feel crushed by his personality, and he would always look on her as his responsibility, as he looked on the station as part of his inheritance, and nothing more.

When the dance ended, and she stood by Ross's side catching her breath, she caught sight of Ella Waden standing by the doorway, accompanied by her father and several of the station hands they had brought with them, and who had evidently just arrived.

Seeing Ella reminded Vicky of Mary's remarks about Ross having a crush on Ella years ago, and her veiled hints about something turning up in that direction, and her spirits lifted. Mary was a shrewd observer, and maybe she knew something about Ross and Ella that Vicky didn't know.

Now, as she watched Ross move forward to greet the Wadens, and heard Mr Waden apologise for their somewhat tardy arrival, explaining that he

had got caught up with a bunch of visitors from
the consortium that owned the station, she took
particular notice of Ross and Ella's attitude towards each other, but disappointingly could detect
no special attraction between them.

Mary's cool remark that Ella still hadn't
married, and making special mention of her age at
the same time, made Vicky feel more hopeful, for
Ella was much too good-looking a girl to be left
on the shelf, not unless she so willed it, for she
could have had her pick of the neighbouring bachelors.

This was not hearsay, it was a plain fact. Vicky
could recall the various events she had attended
during the years, and even though Ella was that
much older than she was, her popularity with the
young bloods of the neighbourhood had been too
marked for anyone to miss, even the tomboyish
Vicky. This was not to say that Ella was a flirt.
Her looks had commanded such attention, and
Vicky, when she had thought about it, had come
to the conclusion that Ella had not always appreciated being made the belle of the ball. It had
invariably made her enemies, and Vicky doubted if
she had any close friends in the female line. Human
nature being what it was, the single girls out for a
husband would be more likely to give Ella a wide
berth.

All this went through Vicky's mind as she looked
at Ella, prettily dressed in a blue and white ging-
ham dress, with a small lacy collar that was not
fussy but just right. Her golden-red hair, that was

naturally curly, was now pulled back in a ponytail, and her smooth, almost too perfect features now relaxed in a smile as she exchanged small talk with Ross.

Vicky's silent observation passed from Ella to her father, who stood by with an indulgent expression on his face as he surveyed his daughter talking to Ross. There was no doubt in Vicky's mind that a match between Ross and his daughter would be welcomed with open arms, and would mean a relaxing of the constant guard Mr Waden had kept on Ella, if all that Vicky had heard was true, and it was said in some quarters that this was the reason for Ella's single status. All admirers, particularly the less endowed ones, were given short shrift by her ambitious father, who did not intend that his beautiful daughter's accomplishments should be wasted on any Tom, Dick or Harry who happened to catch her eye.

Ella, like Vicky, had lost her mother, but at a much earlier age than Vicky, and her father had had to cope with her upbringing, and perhaps this accounted for his almost fanatical over-protective attitude towards his daughter, Vicky thought, as her gaze turned back to Ross, now escorting the party over to the refreshment stand, his height and broad shoulders making his progress through the crowded storeroom easily discernible.

A few minutes later, he led Ella on to the dance floor, giving Vicky ample opportunity to watch out for any sign of affection between them, but try as she might, they were just two friends dancing. The only difference being between the way he had hauled Vicky round the floor and the way he seemed to be taking extra pains not to have his partner bumped into by the less inhibited couples on the floor.

Out of the corner of her eye Vicky saw that Mary was watching her, and they exchanged a confidential look, then Mary grinned and turned her attention to the counter to serve the rest of the Waden party with food.

If she had not been looking in Mary's direction at that particular time, Vicky might have missed making an interesting discovery, for the man standing directly behind Ella's father, and who she knew to be Pete Noonan, Mr Waden's foreman, had his attention firmly fixed on Ross and Ella, in what she could only describe as frustrated fury.

In itself, this was no unusual happening, such was Ella's effect on the male fraternity, but Vicky was surprised to find Pete Noonan adopting such an attitude towards his boss's daughter, for Pete was a ladies' man, whose good looks and smooth manner had created havoc among the local girls, and as Ella could have taken her choice of the bachelors, so Pete could have chosen any one of the local girls. His 'devil-may-care' attitude to life formed a fatal attraction to the opposite sex. All, that was, who did not see beyond his smooth-talking manner and the oversized ego that pushed him relentlessly towards any target he had set his sights on.

As her gaze passed from Pete Noonan and

returned to Ross and Ella, now laughing and catching their breath at the end of the dance, Vicky could not help but feel sorry for Pete Noonan. She did not like him, principally because of the kind of man he was, but if he had fallen at last in love with someone, and that someone was Ella Waden, then there was little chance of a happy ending. Quite apart from the fact that Ella's father would not contemplate such a match, Ella was much too sensible a girl to waste herself on such a man. Of this, Vicky was confident. Possessing beauty had not spoilt Ella, or blinded her to the constant flattery she received; if anything, it had put her just that little bit more on her guard, and a man with a reputation such as Pete had earned would be brushed aside without a second thought.

Shouts for the musicians to play again started up another dance, and Vicky, seeing Ross looking her way, and not wanting another fling around the floor like the last one, started to make tracks for the harbour of the tea counter, but came up against the solid bulk of Pete Noonan, who gave her a sketchy bow and asked for the pleasure of the dance.

Vicky did not want to dance with him, but to refuse would have looked like a snub, and she was feeling sorry for him because she was certain that he was in love with Ella.

Pete had beaten Ross to it by a matter of seconds, and Ross looked none too pleased when Pete led Vicky on to the dancing area. He was even more displeased when, after the dance, Pete stayed persistently by Vicky's side making small conversation about nothing in particular but enough to keep Vicky from making her escape.

Had Vicky really thought about it, she was getting an ideal chance to annoy Ross. As it was, she was too surprised to capitalise on it. Pete Noonan had never bothered with her before, mainly because of Ross, who would have given him his marching orders if he had so much as looked her way, but here he was making a dead set at her, and what was worse, making no effort to conceal the fact.

Far from feeling elated, Vicky knew only embarrassment, and when she saw Ross heading their way with a glint in his eye that spelt trouble for Pete she hastily directed Pete's attention to the refreshment counter and suggested that they have a drink. She would even have suggested they take a walk outside to avoid a head-on collision between the men!

Once at the counter, Vicky slipped behind it and into her serving position, showing her determination to stay put by wrapping herself in Mrs George's apron again.

Pete Noonan was made of sterner stuff, however, and not easily baulked. He was intent on annoying Ross, and was making a good job of it from what Vicky could see, for he stayed put right beside the counter and even helped hand out the tea to Vicky's customers.

One couldn't help but admire his tactics, for without taking Vicky's mind off her job, he managed to convey the impression that he was in-

terested in her. But impression was all it was, and
certainly did not fool Vicky. For some reason,
which wasn't all that hard to guess at, Pete wanted
to get back at Ross, and Vicky was sure Ella had
something to do with it. Her thoughts raced ahead
as she tried to come up with the solution for this
entirely unexpected turn of events, and there was
only one that made sense. Ella must be in love with
Ross—Mary's thoughts on the matter had been
correct. To Pete Noonan's way of thinking Ross
had stolen his girl's heart, and what better way of
revenge than to repay the compliment in kind?

Vicky sighed as she refilled the tea urn. He would
see no obstacle in his way. It was common knowledge that she and Ross would eventually marry. It
must also be common knowledge that it was not a
love match.

Considering everything, it was not a very clever
way of going about things, Vicky thought
shrewdly. Without realising it he was giving Vicky
a hand in her own scheme for her freedom, and
she wondered how he would take it when the
'understanding' between Ross and Vicky was
broken and Ross was free to marry Ella, particularly when he realised that he had paved the
way for them—but that was something that he
wouldn't know until it was too late.

Ross's smooth voice cut across her musings, and
seemed to float across the crowded room towards
them. 'Come on, Noonan. There's some young
ladies here without partners,' he remarked, managing to sound casual, but Vicky knew that he was

giving Pete a clear warning that he was stepping out of his territory.

Pete's equally smooth reply of, 'I like it right here,' as he handed Vicky some used crockery, caused an expectant hush to fall on the crowd, and Vicky tried to pretend she was busy, although she had no customers.

George Waden's authoritative, 'Make like a guest, Pete. We're here to enjoy ourselves. You've no call to disappoint the ladies,' sounded as it was meant to sound, like an order, and for a second or so it looked as if Pete would fail to comply, but after giving a light shrug, he moved away from the counter and started to circulate.

Vicky heaved a sigh of relief as the music started up again. What could have been a nasty moment had been averted by Mr Waden's intervention.

From then on Ross was never far from the refreshment counter, making certain that Vicky was under his watchful eye and once again making her feel like the little sister who had to be protected from the big bad wolf!

The party broke up shortly after one o'clock, which was late, since all the guests were working folk and most of them would have to be up at the crack of dawn to carry out their various duties, but no thought of the morrow could mar the enjoyment of the evening for them, and happily singing parties were sent on their way with a promise from George Waden to hold another in not too distant a future.

Ross's curt 'goodnight' to Vicky as she climbed

into the car after Mary and Jake had taken their seats in the back showed Vicky that he held her partly responsible for encouraging Pete Noonan's attentions, but she took no offence at this silent unfair accusation, for her mind was too busy trying to come to terms with the incredible fact that Pete Noonan intended to go ahead with his scheme of getting at Ross through her.

His quick but unmistakable,' Be seeing you,' as he handed a pile of used crockery to her just before the Waden party had taken their leave, left her in no doubt of this, but she could see nothing but fireworks ahead.

Quite apart from the futility of the scheme, Pete stood a good chance of losing his job, and as her father had remarked, jobs weren't all that easy to come by.

Somehow, she thought disconsolately, she would have to protect him from himself. It was obvious that he wasn't thinking straight, and that meant that he was very much in love with Ella, she thought wearily, even to the point of risking all to get back at Ross.

Her first wish had come true, she thought wistfully, but not at all in the way she had envisaged. Now it looked as if her second wish, to be given her freedom, would also come true, but not in the way she had wanted it, at least not in a way that made trouble for others, and Pete Noonan was heading for trouble with a capital T if he persisted in carrying out his plans.

Why had things to be so awkward? she wondered

wretchedly. All she wanted to do was to free Ross and herself from a binding commitment that neither of them wanted, but it was proving no easy task.

There was Ross's obstinacy for a start, and his fierce pride for a second. It was his pride that would provide the fuel for a battle royal over her—not because he cared for her, but as he himself had said, because he felt responsible for her.

Her brow deepened in thought. If only she knew if Ross really cared for Ella. Or if Ella cared for him.

If they were in love, then it hadn't happened yesterday, she told herself, and they had had ample time to hide their feelings from the rest of the world. If Ross had needed Dale's Creek to provide himself with a decent living, then he could be forgiven for his obstinacy, but he was a wealthy man in his own right and what he was doing he was doing purely through a sense of duty, and it was harder on Ella than on him, and doubly hard on her, had she allowed him to sweep her to the altar.

Only time would tell, she thought, but at least she had given them the opportunity to come out into the open and declare their true feelings.

Her thoughts ran on as she got ready for bed, seeking various ways of coping with what looked like an explosive situation. She could be downright rude to Pete, of course, and give him his marching orders should he make any attempt to contact her, and she just couldn't see herself doing any such thing, but when she recalled the determined way

he had stuck by her side that evening, she knew it
might have to come to that whether she liked it or
not. If it saved him his job, then it would be worth
a little discomfort on her part.

It was all Ross's fault, she thought crossly. If he
hadn't been the kind of man he was, the whole
thing could have been forgotten and passed off as
just a friendly overture on Pete's part, instead of
calling attention to it the way he had, and drawing
everyone's eyes that way, making it into a big
thing.

She sighed as she slipped on her pyjamas after
taking her shower, and got into bed. It was then
that she recalled Mary's comments on their having
to put their heads together where Ross and Ella
were concerned, and she sent a grateful thought
towards Mary, who understood how she felt.

As she put out her bedside light and lay back on
her pillows, she wondered what Mary had in mind.
She hadn't liked the idea at first, and felt that Ross
ought to do his own courting, but it did look as if
he needed a helping hand. Like Pete, he had to be
saved from himself!

Vicky plumped the pillows behind her head and
gave another deep sigh. It was a wonder that any
romance got off the ground, particularly if all the
males were like Ross, whose stiff-necked pride got
in the way of true romance!

As for Mary hoping to manipulate things to
everybody's satisfaction, Vicky couldn't see it happening. Ross liked being in the driving seat and
wouldn't take kindly to any interference in his

affairs. Any such scheme—even if thought up by the shrewd Mary would be spotted a mile away by that hawkeyed maddening man!

Before she fell asleep, Vicky had a vision of Pete Noonan turning up at the homestead and asking for her, and she only hoped that no such an event came to pass.

Her father would reasonably be hoping that his slice of bad luck was over and looking forward to better times. To have Pete Noonan courting his daughter would bring about a relapse, not to mention Ross well and truly on the warpath!

'Really,' she murmured drowsily, 'it's all so unnecessary,' and fell asleep to dream of Ross dressed as an Indian and decked in full warpaint brandishing a tomahawk at some unknown quarry whom she presumed to be Pete Noonan!

CHAPTER SIX

THE following morning, Vicky had a rude awakening in the form of a telephone call from Ross. Her sleepy, 'You can take it for me,' to Mary when she went in to rouse her just after seven, met with, 'he wants to speak to you. Come on—whatever it is it must be important, he wouldn't ring at this time if it wasn't.'

Ross's curt voice soon shook all sleep out of Vicky. 'Mrs George has sprained her ankle pretty badly,' he said brusquely. 'We've had the doctor up and he says she'll have to keep off it for at least a week. I want you up here at the double. You'd better pack a case. You'll be here for a week, if not more,' he stated.

Vicky's eyes opened wide. 'What about Mary coming?' she asked, self-preservation taking over. She didn't want to go.

'Use your sense,' Ross barked back at her. 'She's got Jake and your father to look after. You wanted a job, didn't you? Well, I'm offering you one as temporary housekeeper!' With that he slammed the receiver down on her, leaving her staring at the silent instrument in her hand and thinking of all the things she had wanted to say in reply to that sarcastic remark of his, if she had been given the opportunity.

'Well, what's happened?' Mary asked. 'I heard you offer my services,' she added dryly.

'Which he didn't accept,' Vicky replied sourly. 'Mrs George has sprained her ankle. I don't know how,' she added darkly, and then looked at Mary. 'You don't suppose Ross pushed her down the stairs, do you?' she asked. 'He was pretty furious with me last night—thought I'd encouraged Pete Noonan's attentions.'

'Vicky!' exclaimed Mary in a shocked but amused voice. 'What a thing to say! Of course he didn't! And anyone could see it was Pete doing the chasing. You wouldn't know how to encourage him!' she added with a grin.

'Thank you for your complete confidence in my

being a nincompoop!' Vicky answered crossly. 'As for Ross not doing any such thing, it makes a perfectly good excuse for getting me up to Jarra where he can keep an eye on me, doesn't it?' she added.

'What exactly does he want you to do?' Mary asked with a suspicion of a twinkle in her eye. 'Look after Mrs George?'

'That,' said Vicky, 'will be part of my duties, no doubt. I'm a temporary housekeeper until she's fit.' A thought then struck her and she stared at Mary in consternation. 'Does that mean doing the cooking, too?' she asked with wide eyes.

Mary tried hard not to show her amusement. 'Well, Ross does eat, doesn't he? I hear Mrs George is a first class cook,' she added slyly.

'Thank you!' Vicky exclaimed bitterly. 'That's all I need to make my day! I only hope they own a tin-opener, because that's the limit of my skill in that direction!'

Mary chuckled as she turned back to the kitchen. 'Come and have your breakfast,' she said. 'At least you'll have a good breakfast if no one else at Jarra has.'

A glance at the clock told Vicky that it was seven-fifteen, and if she was expected to get Mrs George's breakfast she had better get a move on. There were things she had to do, packing for instance, although that wouldn't take long. She would need her pyjamas, a change of underwear, and maybe a blouse, she thought disconsolately, as she started on the large helping of bacon and eggs that Mary put before her.

It was at this point that a vision of the kitchen at Jarra loomed before her, particularly the large gleaming oven, and she lost her appetite. 'I'll never manage that oven, Mary,' she said dismally, and then brightened as a thought struck her. 'Perhaps we could cook Mrs George's breakfast here. If I leave as soon as it's ready——?'

Mary shook her head decisively. 'There's nothing worse than cold congealed bacon and eggs, Vicky. For goodness' sake, look on the bright side. Those dials are more for swank than for anything else. Mrs George will tell you how to manage it. You'll get the hang of it in no time, you'll see,' she added confidently.

Vicky wished that she shared that confidence; as it was, she had no such faith in her abilities.

Mary's parting shot, however, as she saw Vicky off fifteen minutes later with, 'Remember, Vicky, the way to a man's heart is through his stomach!' held such amusement in it that Vicky knew that they were both of the same opinion as far as her cooking was concerned.

As she crashed the gears, she called back, 'In that case I've nothing to worry about,' and slid the Holden into action. 'Be seeing you,' she called as the car swept away from the homestead.

On arrival at Jarra, Vicky found Mrs George in her room on the first floor. 'Sorry about this, Vicky,' Mrs George said, and gave a wry grimace. 'It's my own fault really. I ought to have got that loose heel seen to ages ago. I'm lucky that it didn't get caught further up the stairs—as it was, it happened on the last two steps, and apart from wrenching my ankle and a loss of dignity, I'm all right.'

Vicky had never known her so forthcoming. Mrs George was the silent type of woman who rarely indulged in chat, but it did put Vicky at her ease, and she enquired what she would like for breakfast.

'Only toast and tea, please,' Mrs George replied, and gave a smile at Vicky's obvious relief at not having to cook her anything. 'I'm afraid Ross will need something more substantial, though—he'll be in around nine. Three rashers and two eggs should see him right,' she added comfortably.

Vicky tried to look enthusiastic but failed, and was wondering how he'd take to baked beans, if she could find the tin-opener, that was!

'No need to start until about ten to nine,'Mrs George murmured, unaware of Vicky's alternative plans for his breakfast. 'I usually put the bacon under the grill about then and start the eggs a few minutes to nine. It can be put in the plate warmer then ready for serving.'

'I'll need time to work out how that cooker works,' Vicky said carefully, deciding to come clean, it would save a lot of explanation later.

'It's not as bad as all that,' said Mrs George with a smile, 'although I must admit it took me a day or two to get the hang of it when it first came, so I'm sure Ross won't expect too much of you at the start. There's a leaflet in the kitchen drawer giving all the dial positions,' she told Vicky.

After Vicky had taken up Mrs George's tray containing her modest breakfast, Vicky went back to the kitchen and settled down to decipher the oven code, and experiment with the dials.

By ten to nine, she felt capable of producing some sort of a meal, so long as it was not too fancy, she could manage, she thought, and felt reasonably pleased with herself. There was nothing to it, and she wondered why she had got so hot and bothered about the job of taking over from Mrs George. There was bound to be a well-stocked freezer and she could get the menus from Mrs George, all she had to do was to remember to take the stuff out of the freezer in time for the cooking in the evening.

By now the bacon was sizzling merrily in the grill pan, and as it was a few minutes to nine, Vicky put the eggs on. Any minute now Ross would make his appearance, and he wouldn't have anything to complain about, Vicky thought happily as she turned her attention back to the cooker manual. There was something that she hadn't quite grasped about the timer, an ingenious mechanism that allowed you to leave the food cooking in the oven and would switch itself off when it was ready. The oven at Dale's Creek possessed no such refinement, although Vicky could see what a boon it would be to a busy housewife.

A quick glance at the clock told her it was a quarter past nine, and she frowned. Mrs George had said nine o'clock, hadn't she? Perhaps she had better check, she thought, and leaving the eggs nicely frying on a low heat, and the grill also turned down low, she slipped up to Mrs George's room. 'You did say nine o'clock, didn't you?' she asked, just putting her head round the door and not going in to save time.

'Not back yet?' Mrs George asked. 'Oh, well, I expect he's got held up. Just as long as it's ready when he comes,' she commented comfortably. 'Do you want to take my tray down?' she queried.

Vicky had only just got back to the kitchen when Ross came in. His first glance went to the kitchen table and seeing that his place had not yet been laid, frowned. 'Late in getting here, were you?' he asked pithily.

'I've been here since eight o'clock!' Vicky exclaimed indignantly. 'And you were supposed to be here at nine,' she added crossly, as she began to dish up the now rather over-cooked breakfast and put it down in front of him with a firm thump, then found the cutlery and put that beside him, then went over to the dresser and put two slices of bread in the toaster. She might have known something would go wrong, she thought angrily.

It took her a minute to realise that Ross had not exactly fallen on his plate the way a hungry man was expected to, and glancing back at him, she saw that he was making experimental jabs with his fork at the eggs. 'What did you cook them in—rubber solution?' he asked, adding sarcastically, 'I haven't seen bacon like that since my schooldays when we were out on the bush trail. Is that toast I can smell burning?' he asked, adding insult to injury, and making Vicky want to scream at him, but she would take him up on that later, she thought darkly. Right now she had to scrape the charred remains out of the toaster. Mrs George had told her to watch the toaster, it was apt to burn the bread as it had a faulty switch.

It was Ross who finally got his own breakfast, and to Vicky's chagrin, wouldn't even allow her to make the coffee, throwing away the over-stewed liquid and making a fresh pot. 'Just,' he said grimly, 'look after Mrs George. She can afford indigestion, I'm too busy!'

An affronted Vicky left him to it, and went to get her orders from Mrs George. There had to be something she could do, she thought scathingly, and if Ross had wanted a cook, then he should have sent for Mary, not her!

Only after Ross had gone did Vicky venture downstairs again. Mrs George had given her a list of light duties to perform. The heavy work was carried out by two of the station wives who took turns in helping out.

Mrs George had also given her a menu for lunch around twelve-thirty, the time Ross would usually put in another appearance, but when Vicky got back to the kitchen it was evident that he had provided himself with sandwiches, not, she thought darkly, prepared to take a chance on what she had to offer.

Well, that was fine by her, she thought airily, and she only hoped that he would keep the practice up! All she would have to worry about then was the evening meal and she had all day to prepare it. Perhaps she might surprise him with a passable offering!

Mary rang shortly after she had taken Mrs George her mid-morning cup of coffee and was just settling down to have hers. 'Pete Noonan rang,' Mary said. 'I told him you were at Jarra. He said, "Okay" and rang off. You're not going to tangle with him, are you, Vicky?' she asked, sounding worried. 'You know what he's like. He's a regular flirt, and Ross wouldn't like it.'

Vicky muttered something under her breath about Ross lumping it, and at Mary's 'What was that?' replied calmly, 'Don't worry, Mary, I'm not stupid.'

'I know you're not,' Mary said slowly, 'but he's jealous of Ross. Most of them are,' and left the rest unfinished, but Vicky knew what she meant.

'You mean it's not my fatal attraction that's caused his apparent lapse from sanity, don't you?' she queried sweetly.

Mary chuckled. 'Since you put it like that,' she said, highly amused, 'that's just what I did mean, although I might have known you wouldn't be taken in. How are you getting on?' she asked, suddenly changing the subject.

'Ross asked if I'd fried the eggs in rubber solution,' Vicky replied, and at Mary's howl of laughter continued in a dignified voice, 'It's not my fault if he's fifteen minutes late, is it? I think he's beginning to come to the same conclusion as me!' she added meaningly, knowing that Mary would know what she was referring to.

'Oh, dear,' gasped Mary, recovering from her amusement. 'Look, how about if I pop up this afternoon? Jake could bring me. I could prepare a dinner for you. It's Mrs George I'm thinking of,' she added, making matters worse for Vicky.

'Mrs George, according to Ross, can afford indigestion,' Vicky replied coldly, 'and I've found the tin-opener, thank you.'

'Are you sure?' Mary persisted. 'It's no trouble for me.'

'If you come, I'm the one who's in trouble,' Vicky replied. 'I did offer your services to Ross and got my head bitten off for my trouble—no, you stay put. I like things as they are.'

Ross put in an appearance shortly after Mary had rung off. 'I've a meeting here tonight,' he told Vicky, and at her scowl at the thought of having to prepare food for them, added sarcastically, 'Don't worry, they're coming after dinner. I suppose there will be dinner?' he asked silkily.

Vicky did not reply but just stood glaring at him. There was a lot she could say, but she knew who would have the last word! To think that once she was supposed to marry him! The very idea was not only ludicrous, it was mind-boggling!

'Have a word with Mrs George,' he went on blandly. 'She'll tell you what to get ready for the meeting. She's a good cook, too,' he added maddeningly, 'you couldn't get a better training.'

Vicky didn't see why he had to bring that up again. 'We can't all be good cooks,' she replied furiously, 'and I've a feeling my talents lie in other directions!'

'After this morning's showing, I'm inclined to agree with you,' Ross remarked smoothly, but there was a trace of amusement in his eyes that annoyed Vicky more than a lecture would have done. 'Mrs George usually prepares some canapés,' he added, 'but you can put some biscuits and cheese out if you can't manage anything more fancy. Anyway, have a word with her. There'll be six of us, all told.'

To Vicky's immense relief he turned to go, but as he got to the door he turned back to her. 'Watch out for Pete Noonan,' he said casually. 'If he starts hanging around, tell me. I'll soon settle his hash,' he added meaningly.

Vicky felt a surge of fury at this autocratic order. 'Thank you,' she replied angrily, 'but that's my business.'

Ross's blue eyes narrowed, and he walked slowly back into the room. 'So he has pestered you,' he said softly.

Vicky drew in a deep breath. 'That's your interpretation,' she said angrily, 'and it's not mine. It's nothing to do with you.'

'Do you know what kind of a man Pete Noonan is?' Ross shouted at her.

Vicky felt an overwhelming urge to grin, her fury dispelled at Ross's loss of temper, and turned her face away, carefully studying the black and white tiled floor at her feet. 'You mean he's a ladies' man, don't you?' she said slowly, hoping that her amusement did not show in her voice, but she did not allow for Ross's almost uncanny way of knowing her every mood.

'Think it's funny, do you?' he asked harshly, 'or are you looking for a little experience? If it's experience, then you've sure got the right man. If you think he's fallen for you, then you'd better think again. He's out to have a go at me, and that's all there is to it. It's so damned obvious a child could see through his tactics, and so will everyone else. If you want to make a fool of yourself, then go ahead, but don't expect any sympathy from me when he gets tired of the game,' he told her savagely.

Vicky was feeling savage herself. She knew she was not a beauty, but why did everyone have to underline the fact? Was she so unattractive that no man would look at her for any other reason than the one he had just outlined? Even if it was the truth, she hadn't needed telling.

'Of course I know he hasn't fallen for me,' she said coldly. 'I'm not that dumb—and yes, I'd guessed there was more to it, but girls like me don't very often get a chance of flirting with a good-looking man, do they?' she asked sweetly. 'I'm quite looking forward to it,' she added grimly. 'Don't worry, I know what I'm doing. I won't come crying on your shoulder when it's all over,' she tacked on airily, in spite of the fury that was welling up inside her.

'I don't believe you know what flirting means,' Ross said caustically, 'and I'm damn sure you're in for a shock. I guess it's up to me to enlighten you,' and he pulled the unsuspecting Vicky into his arms, clamping her slight body to his hard one, reminding her of the last time he had made a grab at her.

Vicky had not been in the mood then, and she certainly was not in the mood for another demonstration now, and she struggled furiously to free herself. 'What do you think you're doing?' she got out breathlessly.

Ross ignored her furious attempts to break free from him and his hard blue eyes roamed over her flushed countenance. 'He'll hold you tight—like this,' he said softly, 'only I don't suppose he'll expect to meet with any opposition, he's not used to it,' he murmured in a silky voice. 'Not that that would deter him. In fact it will probably spur him on. Some men like a challenge.'

Vicky felt his arms tighten around her, and knew a sense of panic. In some indefinable way she knew he was not referring to Pete Noonan but to himself, and was thoroughly enjoying frightening her, only she was not going to show him that she was frightened, she thought, but her thudding heart belied her bravado. All she had to remember was that this was Ross, the man she had known all her life, and who was now amusing himself at her expense.

'He'll then steal a kiss,' Ross went on remorselessly, and at Vicky's deliberate action to avoid his lips, he placed his hand under her chin and made her look up at him. It was like being caught in a vice, she thought, for there was no escape. Then he swiftly kissed her. 'Of course, there's an art in kissing,' he said softly against her lips, and gently teased the corners of her soft mouth, tracing their outline with slow deliberation.

Vicky felt shivers go down her back. This was nothing like the swift, almost impersonal kiss he had given her back at Dale's Creek a few days ago, and she was ashamed to admit that she liked it, and she had a nasty feeling that soon she wouldn't want him to stop.

Her feelings were so unexpected that for a moment she was off her guard and her stiff body relaxed gently against him.

'That's better,' said Ross in a low voice, pulling her even closer to him. 'Now let me kiss you properly.'

Vicky felt mesmerised. She didn't know what was happening to her, she only knew that when Ross had teased the corners of her lips she had wanted a real kiss. She lifted her face to him, her large brown eyes fixed on his firm lips, and as they descended on hers, her bones turned to jelly, and her arms slid round his neck in an entirely abandoned action as she went deeper into the whirlpool of emotion, not caring about the future but only living for this moment in time.

When Ross ended the kiss, he stood looking down at her brightly flushed features and eyes that had a stunned expression in them, his eyes narrowed. 'I think that's enough for a start,' he said harshly. 'Proves my point, though, doesn't it? You could no more handle a petting session than fly a jet. A man like Noonan would know that in five seconds flat,' he added savagely. 'I only hope you keep some sense of values,' he flung back at her, before he stamped out of the homestead.

Vicky stood transfixed. She felt as if she had been slapped hard in the face. She had made the most colossal fool of herself—correction, Ross Janson had made a fool of her—and she had just stood by and let him do it!

Bright tears of frustration clouded her eyes. How she hated him! If Pete Noonan was a ladies' man, he had a long way to go before he measured up to the sort of performance she had just been subjected to!

Her soft lips twisted ironically; he had said that he was no ladies' man! She had certainly learned a hard lesson, but she had learned something else. There was more to Ross Janson than met the eye!

She thought of Ella. No wonder she was still single. If Ross had 'played' with her, as he had with Vicky, it was small wonder that she had not looked at any other man!

A wave of sympathy for Ella washed over her, and a further surge of hatred of Ross. He hadn't been able to resist giving her what he termed as a lesson, and thoroughly enjoying himself at the same time. Thank heaven she didn't love him, she thought gratefully—but she might well have done, she thought musingly, and what havoc he would have been able to play in her life.

She nodded her head thoughtfully. Yes, she was glad she had come to Jarra. She had to find out some time that the man she had once thought of as a kindly kind of brother was capable of being cruel.

He knew she was inexperienced, and there were other ways of preparing her for a wolf's advances, other than a physical demonstration like the one he had just given her, and if she were not very careful he would follow it up, given half a chance, but she did not intend to place herself at his mercy again.

She frowned as the thought suddenly struck her that there wouldn't be much she could do about it if he had set his mind on educating her in this line.

When she recalled the way he had grabbed her at Dale's Creek that day, when he had still been of the opinion that they should marry, a cold shiver went up her back. Yes, he was capable of weakening her resistance if he set his mind to it, she thought wretchedly.

He had not shown her any consideration then either, but used her as a piece of merchandise that he owned and could do what he liked with.

She also recalled what he had said to her that same evening, too. How he had held off making advances to her before as he felt she was not ready for them, and his harsh condemnation of her when he had said he wanted a helpmate, not a stupid chit of a girl for a wife—or words to that affect, she thought, and shook her head slowly. That was just as well, she told herself. This stupid chit of a girl is not so stupid. She had his measure for one thing, and a strong sense of preservation for another!

It was going to be this preservation that would save her pride, that ought by now to be in tatters, bullied as she was by someone she used to look up to.

She felt a sense of indignation that her father had been so keen on the match that he had not thought to give the matter any serious consideration, but then he had not seen the other side of Ross. He only knew him as a friend and the son of a man he had liked and respected for years.

That, thought Vicky wearily, was all very well, but hardly a good enough reason for putting his daughter in the firing line, amalgamation or no amalgamation!

CHAPTER SEVEN

If Vicky had given way to her feelings at that time, she would have walked out of Jarra, but there was Mrs George to consider, and she had more sense than to give in to what would have been a childish impulse on her part.

She had let Ross get the better of her emotions, and whatever else she did, she refused to give him the satisfaction of knowing how wretched he had made her feel.

That she was vulnerable had been proved beyond question, but only because she was inexperienced, she argued silently with herself. It looked as if she was a slow developer, and that was what Ross had thought, and why he had not pushed the question of marriage even though she was nineteen, almost twenty, she thought miserably.

Taking a deep breath, she straightened her slim shoulders and shook off an almost uncontrollable urge to weep her heart out. She didn't know why she felt so weak and so disturbed. Something had happened to her while Ross was kissing her, and as yet she had not been able to clarify the feeling. That she had enjoyed the sensation of the kiss she could not deny. She hadn't wanted the kiss to end and had wanted it to go on. A lovely soporific feeling stole over her at the memory, and a slight flush stained her cheeks.

If that was flirting, then she liked it! She felt better for coming to this conclusion. It was nothing to get upset about. There was so much she did not know and, up until now, had not wanted to know. Now, however, things were different, and if Pete Noonan did ring and wanted to take her out, she would accept the invitation. She would not get a better chance to get her own back on Ross, she decided.

When she delivered Ross's message to Mrs George about the meeting that evening, she was given directions as to how to set the drinks tray out and to make sure that there was enough whisky and beer in the cabinet, and if not, where the stocks were kept. As for the canapés, Mrs George had given a lift of her bushy eyebrows. 'We haven't had canapés for ages,' she said. 'Most of the men

prefer cheese and biscuits, they're too busy discussing whatever project they've got on hand to
bother with any fancy concoction.'

Her eyes looked amused as she looked at Vicky.
'I think Ross is having a little game with you,' she
said. 'He probably wants to see what kind of a
show you'll put on,' she added musingly. 'Canapés
are a left-over from Mrs Janson's time. She was
very keen on them. I used to go to endless trouble
preparing them for parties, they're a bit fiddly,' she
confided, with a smile.

Vicky wished she had known all this before and
could have asked Ross why he had suddenly
decided to give his guests canapés. However, it
proved again that he was amusing himself at her
expense, and she very nearly asked Mrs George to
tell her how to make the canapés, but thought
better of it. She was not out to please him in any
way, and he would be really amused if she tried
and failed.

The dinner was the next item on the agenda, and
Mrs George provided Vicky with a menu that did
not entail too much preparation—a steak and
kidney pie, already made by Mrs George a few days
earlier, which had only to be taken out of the deep
freeze a few hours before cooking. There were
plenty of fresh vegetables to be had, or failing that,
the freezer was well stocked with whatever Vicky
fancied to add to the menu. The same went for the
sweet, and Vicky could choose from a number of
fruit pies in the freezer, although Mrs George suggested an apple pie as Ross was particularly fond

of her home-baked ones, and would eat it either hot or cold, with or without embellishment—which was just as well, Vicky thought dryly, for that was how he was getting it.

As there was a meeting that evening, dinner would be half an hour earlier, Mrs George said. The meeting usually started around seven, so she advised Vicky to have the dinner ready by six o'clock.

The insistent ringing of the telephone sent Vicky downstairs again, and when she answered it, she was not at all surprised to hear Pete Noonan's voice on the other end of the line. 'Hi, gorgeous!' he said lazily. 'Said I'd be in touch. Got anything on tonight?' he asked casually.

Vicky was still getting over being called 'gorgeous', and wondered how Mrs George would have appreciated being so called. 'How did you know it was me?' she asked, more for playing for time than for curiosity.

He chuckled. 'She's got her foot up, hasn't she? News travels fast on the two-way radio. Well?' he asked.

'What have you got in mind?' Vicky asked cautiously.

'Nothing special,' Pete replied. 'We have a social club up here. We're allowed to invite guests— thought you'd like to come up.'

Vicky thought that over. At least they would not be alone. She knew most of the station hands and their wives, and there wouldn't be any harm in spending an evening with them. 'All right,' she said quickly. 'What time shall I come?'

'I'll collect you,' he replied in a pleased voice.
'Say around seven?'

It couldn't be better, Vicky thought, as she put
the phone down. Ross would be settling down to
his meeting by then and could cause no awkward-
ness. Mrs George had said that the meetings went
on for hours, and she ought to be back before the
meeting broke up. Even if she wasn't, it wouldn't
matter. It was not as if she was going behind Ross's
back, she was free now and could please herself
who she went out with.

Vicky went about her various duties with a
happy feeling that at last things were going right
for her, and it was not until some time later that
she realised that she would have to go back to
Dale's Creek some time before that evening to collect something to wear for her evening out with
Pete. She couldn't possibly go as she was. Her old
jeans were freshly laundered, but they were still
shabby, and her checked shirtwaister was now
faded to a ghost of its former bright colours.

She sighed. It would mean running the gauntlet
with Mary, who never missed anything. She would
be sure to put two and two together and get the
sum right. That meant a lecture. Vicky's chin went
out. It was about time she was allowed to do what
she wanted to do without being treated as if she
was fresh out of kindergarten!

Having taken the pies out of the freezer and left
them to defreeze in good time for dinner, Vicky,
after providing Mrs George with a light salad

lunch, and being assured that she would be all right
for an hour or so, as she would settle down for her
usual after-lunch nap and saw no reason why Vicky
should not slip back to Dale's Creek to collect a
few odds and ends that she had forgotten to bring
with her, for that was how Vicky had put it, there
had been no need for any other explanation.

Back at Dale's Creek, Vicky found Mary washing up the lunch dishes and at her surprised, 'What
are you doing back?' she explained carefully that
there were a few things she needed and had not
had time to pack properly that morning.

After giving her a hard look, Mary accepted her
reason for her return, but Vicky had an idea that
she knew very well why Vicky had returned and
what clothes she had forgotten to pack, but to her
relief Mary made no comment, and she made her
way to her room before anything else could be
said.

Still feeling as if she was working against time,
Vicky threw her best velvet trews and two of her
nicest blouses into what had been her mother's
overnight case, and on an afterthought tucked in
the vanity case that Aunt May had given her for
her seventeenth birthday and that contained some
make-up which she hoped was still usable. Then
finding the finely made moccasins that she kept for
special occasions, she was on her way again, calling
out, 'Cheerio,' to Mary as she went out of the
door.

Mary's veiled warning of, 'You take care,'
followed her out of the house, showing Vicky that

she had got her sums right, and it did occur to her that she might just give her father a hint of the company his daughter was keeping, and she knew what would happen then. He would lose no time in contacting Ross. Her brow darkened. She would never forgive Mary for letting her down, if she did.

A few miles farther on from Dale's Creek, Vicky relaxed and gave an amused smile. She didn't know what she was worried about. After this evening everyone would know that she and Ross had split up. It meant a few lectures all round, but she was prepared for that. There would be no need for her to see Pete again either, it was a case of mission accomplished, and it was too bad if Pete had other ideas, for she had no intention of becoming further embroiled with him.

At dinner that evening, Ross had no complaint to make about her cooking. Which considering everything was not surprising, for all she had had to do was put it in the oven and take it out when it was ready, then serve it up!

The only disagreement arose when Vicky had wanted to have her meal with Mrs George, for she felt that she ought to make some effort to give her some company. Up until now there hadn't been much time for gossip between them, but Ross would not hear of her taking her meal with her. 'Mrs George likes to listen to the news around now, and she won't thank you for making small talk,' he had said firmly, and that was that.

He was surprisingly good-humoured during the meal, and Vicky was tempted to fall back into their old companionable relationship again, but the memory of what had taken place that morning was too vivid, and she found herself occasionally stealing a swift look at him when she thought he was not looking, much as one would do to a new acquaintance, as if trying to gauge their personality without being too obvious about it.

'Don't worry, I'm not going to make a grab at you,' Ross said, after Vicky sent him another of her surreptitious glances, proving that he had been aware of them all the time and making her want to throw the condiments at him. 'I'm too busy this evening,' he said airily. 'Besides, I believe in small doses for a start, anyway,' he added, his eyes showing his amusement at Vicky's fury.

'Chance would be a fine thing!' Vicky spat out at him. 'You'll not catch me napping a second time!'

'Want a bet on it?' Ross said silkily, one autocratic eyebrow shooting up in a mock challenge.

Vicky let the challenge pass. She knew it would be a waste of breath to argue with him in that mood, instead she asked him if he was ready for his sweet, and this further amused him as he acknowledged her refusal to take up the challenge.

After the meal, Vicky saw to the dishes, and got everything ready for the meeting which was being held in the dining room, the large circular table being used as the conference table. She had earlier prepared some crackers and buttered them, then cut up some squares of cheese and as directed by Mrs George, placed them on dishes ready to be laid out beside the drinks tray.

When all was ready, she slipped up to see Mrs George. She had not as yet told her that she would be out that evening, and felt mean at walking out on her on her first day at Jarra, but she hoped that she would understand. It was not as if she was helpless. She could move around on her own and was not absolutely dependent upon her.

Vicky found her engrossed in some tapestry work, and listening to the radio, and when Vicky told her that she had made arrangements to go out that evening, sounding as apologetic as she felt, Mrs George quickly reassured her. 'I'm used to my own company,' she told Vicky. 'Ross is more out than in, and if I'd wanted company I'd have left years ago,' she added with a smile. 'My radio is all I need, and I occasionally listen in on the open lines. You go ahead.'

Her assurance relieved Vicky, for she knew that she was speaking the truth. Her own life had been the same as Mrs George's, and she had been quite content to make her own amusements. Vicky then offered to make her a flask of coffee, but Mrs George told her that she would not be needing anything else until much later, and that she would appreciate a pot of tea as a nightcap when Vicky got back.

All that Vicky had to do now was to get ready for her evening out. She hadn't a great deal of time, fifteen minutes in fact, but it did not take her long to have a quick shower and change into her other clothes.

After a quick look at the make-up she had brought back with her, she was pleasantly surprised to find it was still usable. With a little dab of powder on her face and a touch of lipstick that was not too bright, she felt equal to what she hoped would be an evening of enjoyment.

By now it was a few minutes to seven, and she was determined to meet Pete in the drive of the homestead, seeing all kinds of trouble ahead if he walked up to the homestead and asked for her.

Her fond imaginings of being able to slip out of the front door without encountering Ross were shattered by his, 'Where do you think you're going?' as she got to the door.

'Just out for a walk,' lied Vicky, wondering why she had been so unfortunate as to get caught. A second later and she would have been out of the door, but he just had to pass through the hallway at that particular time.

'Dressed like that?' Ross queried softly. 'And with that muck on your face? I'm sure you can do better than that,' he added meaningly.

'I'm only taking your advice and doing something about my appearance,' Vicky retorted sweetly. 'You ought to congratulate me for listening to you,' she added acidly.

'If you're doing what I think you're doing, then I'll tan the hide off you,' he growled. 'And you can take that innocent look off your face, and that stuff you've put on. Who are you meeting?' he shot out at her, then his eyes narrowed, and he gave a low whistle. 'I didn't think he'd have the nerve,' he said softly. 'Outside, is he? Well, we'll both meet him,' and he wrenched the door open, giving Vicky no chance of running for it by holding her arm in a steel grip.

At this precise moment the telephone rang, and Vicky could see that he was torn between answering it, or settling Pete's hash, as he would have put it.

To her relief the call won the tussle, mainly because he didn't want to disturb Mrs George.

Vicky needed no second chance and was out of the door as Ross lifted the receiver, utterly disregarding his furious, 'You stay right where you are!'

Once outside, she ran down the drive, and saw Pete just getting out of his car. She hurried towards it and without any more ado got into the passenger seat, saying breathlessly, 'Let's get out of here—I'll explain later.'

When the car had moved far enough away from the homestead, and Vicky was able to catch her breath, she realised what a ridiculous start they had made to the evening. She couldn't have sounded more panic-stricken if she had just robbed a bank and the law was hot on her trail, and felt an irresistible urge to giggle, although it was not really funny.

'Big brother on the warpath?' asked Pete, and Vicky caught the white flash of his teeth as he grinned appreciatively at the thought.

'Not exactly,' she replied carefully. 'It's just that things are a bit awkward,' she ended lamely, feeling a traitor, because Ross had her welfare at heart even if he had a funny way of showing it.

Pete shot her a quick sideways look. 'Time you stood up for yourself,' he said musingly. 'You'll never know what's what otherwise,' he added meaningly.

Vicky's ears pricked up at this, although she gave no sign that she was interested. Did he mean that there was something between Ella and Ross? she wondered. As she was not certain, she kept silent hoping for more information, but she was disappointed, for Pete confined the conversation to more general topics, remarking how colourful the wattle bushes were, and how he would never settle to live in the town.

As Vicky's eyes followed his, out to the golden bushes of the wattle that was Australia's emblem, she felt the same way, and wondered how she could ever have contemplated living in the confines of a town. Early summer was the best time of all, she thought. The grasslands around them had been cleared of natural woodland to the extent that there was a free run for the sheep broken only by an occasional mallee eucalyptus tree, and small groups of 'grass trees', dotted here and there, gave the impression of parkland rather than working stations. This was what man had created out of woodland and thick forest, and to Vicky, the loveliest part of the south-west, but then she was biased, this was her home.

As her eyes lingered over the sheep she could see roaming up the slopes ahead of them, now shorn of their thick coats and looking startlingly white against the growing dusk of the evening, she forgot that only a week ago she had wanted to leave all this behind her and start a new life, and would have been surprised if reminded of it, for no such thoughts were in her mind now.

This was still Jarra land, and ten miles farther on they came to the boundaries of the Albury station, given the name simply because it had been bought up by a consortium of business men from Albury, and not because of its location. Of the three stations, Dale's Creek was the nearest to the town, being a mere fifteen miles away, Jarra and the Albury station adding a further ten and five miles respectively, distances which were mere pinpricks to the vast acreage of a grazier's station.

Seen on a map, the three stations formed a triangle with their lands meeting on three sides of their boundaries. Dale's Creek and Jarra homesteads forming the base of the triangle and only fifteen miles apart were practically back to back. With good roads and no traffic as such, the distance could be traversed easily and caused no problems.

It was a long time since Vicky had been to Ella's home, and she was struck by the various changes she saw. The homestead that she could see in the distance had undergone various alterations. A huge wooden structure had been added to the southern side of the homestead and was obviously offices. It now looked exactly what it was, a big business expansion rather than a homestead, and Vicky wondered what Ella thought about that. Not that she or her father would have any say in the matter, but at least they had a roof over their heads, even if it didn't belong to them any more.

These thoughts reminded Vicky of her own situation. Dale's Creek didn't belong to a Dale any more either, and was now Ross Janson's property. If Ross did the same to Dale's Creek as the consortium had done to the Waden property, Vicky didn't think she could bear it. Perhaps she ought to marry him, she mused; she might just be able to talk him out of any such plans. This last thought pulled her out of her reverie. What was she doing even dreaming of such a thing! As if Ross would take any notice of her wishes—he would do exactly what he wanted to do, and that was that.

Pete swung the car past the homestead and round to a group of buildings at the back, then pulled into a makeshift parking lot and drew to a stop. 'It's nothing fancy,' he said as he got out of the car. 'Just home from home, and it gives the boys somewhere to go of an evening. The consortium had it built a year ago—didn't spare the amenities either. We've a pool table as well as a full sized bar, as you'll see,' he added, as he went to assist Vicky to alight, but she jumped nimbly out. Whatever else could be levelled at Pete Noonan, he knew his manners she thought, as she walked beside him into the social club.

Vicky had been all set for a nice evening among friends, but even this, like all her plans recently, went slightly awry. What had been a happy sociable gathering settled into a hush of tense expectancy at their arrival. The atmosphere was electric and could have been cut with a knife; it was anything but a happy welcome.

It took Vicky a little time to work out the reason for her sudden unpopularity—not only hers but Pete's as well. It was too marked to be put down to her imagination, and however hard she tried to ignore the way everyone seemed to be engrossed in their own conversation to the exclusion of Vicky and Pete, the message was too marked to be missed.

After an uncomfortable ten minutes in which Vicky tried to show an interest in the Babycham Pete had got her, and the light conversation that he kept up to put her at her ease, he gave it up. 'Let's get out of here,' he said abruptly. 'I guess we're not welcome.'

As he led her out of the club and towards his car, Vicky wondered where else they could go, but she got into the car and waited for him to join her, telling herself that if he suggested that they go to his quarters, then it was definitely no go!

'Don't want to worry your pretty head about that,' he said comfortably as he got in the car. 'Some folks are just petty-minded,' and he started up the car.

In spite of the heaviness he had tried to put into his voice, Vicky sensed that he was not displeased at their cold reception. 'I'm not worried,' she replied dryly. 'I'm not pretty, either,' she added. 'I know you're out to annoy Ross and I think I know why, so we'll go from there. I'm not too struck on Ross myself right now,' she tacked on meaningly.

Pete gave her a sideways look. 'You know something? You're pretty cute,' he said quickly.

'I'm not cute,' Vicky retorted, 'and I'm not stupid. If anything, it's common sense. Where are we going?' she asked as she saw that they were heading towards the town.

'Don't underrate yourself,' Pete replied in an amused voice. 'I said you're cute and I meant it. You'd be surprised how many other guys think so too. Trouble with you is you've never bothered to look more than sixteen, and with that baby face of yours, you've got away with it, but you won't be able to sidestep attention for long. If Janson doesn't buck his ideas up he'll be pipped at the post,' he added, as he turned off the main road and down an old track. 'I thought we'd pay a visit to old Hansome. He's got a wonderful collection of antique saddles,' he explained, replying to Vicky's question.

'I suppose he'll let us in?' Vicky said ironically, deciding to ignore the compliment Pete had just paid her, he knew how to flatter a girl, and she wasn't going to be taken in like that. 'We're not exactly top of the popularity poll, are we?' she added dryly.

Now she was certain that Pete was enjoying himself for he gave a deep chuckle. 'Oh, sure he will. Old Handsome just likes to talk. He'll be too busy showing off his treasures to worry about anything else,' he said.

The rest of the drive was taken in silence, each busy with their thoughts. The fact that Pete had accepted her refusal to take his attention seriously proved that she had been right in her original thinking. If anything, he was probably relieved, she thought. If you were in love with someone, it couldn't be easy trying to make up to someone else. She thought of Ella's stunning good looks and wondered how Pete could have expected her to believe his blarney about her, Vicky's, attractions.

Her thoughts ran on. In her mind's eye she could still see the expressions on the station hands' faces when they had looked at her. Incredulity, embarrassment—it was all there, and downright dislike when they had looked at Pete. He had broken a code of honour, stolen someone else's girl. She shot a quick look at Pete, now pulling up outside a shanty type of building in a smallholding where the snorts of pigs could be heard emitting from a ramshackle building a little farther up from the shack. Did he realise that when the news got around he could possibly lose his job? she wondered. If he did lose his job, then it would be her fault, she thought miserably. She had been too busy planning her revenge on Ross to realise the outcome of her evening out.

If she had ever been inclined to doubt Ross's popularity with his neighbours, then she had certainly received confirmation that evening. It wasn't a question of being on the boss's side either. All those men were Albury men, and as for their wives—Vicky's soft lips twisted ironically. Sarah

Downs had actually spilt her drink down her nice blue blouse in complete astonishment at seeing Vicky being escorted by Pete Noonan. What had started out as a nice cosy evening had turned into a farce without the laughter. The wires would be humming with the news by now, and tomorrow the whole area would be aware of Vicky's defection.

With one hit she had scored a bullseye! she thought, and immediately brightened. She didn't know why she had always to look on the dark side of things. As for Pete, he was big enough to look out for himself, and surely he could not have been so blind as to miss the possible consequences of his actions.

Vicky decided to enjoy herself for what was left of the evening. There would be no more dates with Pete, he knew she was wise to him. Each in their own way had had a score to settle with Ross, and it was now settled. Vicky had flown her flag of independence and meant to keep it flying.

As Pete had surmised, they were welcomed with open arms by the old-timer, who was soon showing them round his collection of saddles, and odd bric-à-brac collected over a number of years, including a small nugget of gold handed down from a great-grandfather of his who had been in the gold rush of the 1850s.

It was ten o'clock before they were allowed to leave, and even then the old man was still talking to them as they waved him farewell, promising to return at a later date, at which Vicky felt rather mean, since she knew the visit would not be repeated, at least not with Pete, who he had assumed was her beau.

With the comfortable feeling that Ross's meeting was still in full swing, for when Mrs George had said that it went on for hours she had taken her at her word, there had been enough of them for her to know what she was talking about, Vicky relaxed on the way home. She had enjoyed listening to the old man, and his exhibits were unique. It was a pity that he was so far off the beaten track, for she felt that many more people would enjoy a visit, and it was plain that he enjoyed company.

On reaching Jarra, Vicky thanked Pete for the evening out. She had asked him to drop her at the drive-in entrance to the homestead, taking no chance of meeting any of the members of the meeting as they left Jarra.

'Thanks for your company,' said Pete, as he slowed the car to a stop. 'Believe it or not, I sure enjoyed the evening,' and before Vicky could stop him he had leaned towards her and given her a swift kiss on the lips.

Vicky got out of the car, and turning to give him an impersonal wave of the hand made her way up the bush bordered drive to the homestead.

Her first thought was to get in, and safely up to her room without encountering Ross, and when she saw that the lights were still on in the dining room, she gave a sigh of relief. The meeting was still on, although it was now almost eleven o'clock, and considering the distances some of the members must have come, it would certainly be a late evening for them.

She was about to slip up to her room when she remembered her promise to Mrs George, and had to change direction and go to the kitchen to make the pot of tea she had promised her, on edge all the time in case Ross came upon her.

For once luck was on her side, and as she got to Mrs George's door with the tray of tea and biscuits, she heard Ross's deep voice calling 'goodnight' to his companions, and as it was unlikely that he would call on Mrs George at that time of night, she knew that she was home and dry.

CHAPTER EIGHT

VICKY'S certainty that Ross would not call on Mrs George proved a fallacy, for as she was about to slip out to the shower room she heard him talking to Mrs George. He had not gone into her room but stood outside, enabling Vicky to hear what was said, and she heard him ask Mrs George if she, Vicky, had returned, and when Mrs George had assured him of this, he had said goodnight to her, and went downstairs again.

It was small wonder that he hadn't actually looked in her room to ascertain that she was in, Vicky thought crossly, and felt like the junior of the household who had to be back in the fold before everybody else could retire for the night.

Just before she went to sleep that night, she remembered Pete's kiss. Odd, really, she thought, but she couldn't say that she had enjoyed it. She hadn't expected him to kiss her, but that did not alter the fact that he had, and even in those brief moments when his lips were on hers, she experienced none of the emotions that Ross's kiss had evoked in her. 'I guess some people have it, and some haven't,' she murmured drowsily before sleep claimed her.

She was woken the following morning by the sound of Ross's Land Rover starting up, and she saw that it was just after six. Ross believed in getting an early start, she thought, and lay back on her pillows. No one had said what time she should start work, if that was what it was called, and perhaps she had been lucky that Ross hadn't demanded some sustenance before he started work, and hauled her out of it.

As she was wide awake now, Vicky decided to get up. Today would be a day of reckoning with Ross, she was quite sure of that. He was not likely to forget the way she had taken advantage of that phone call and run out on him at a time when his hands were tied by the meeting.

When Vicky took Mrs George her morning tea, she found her still in bed and listening to the radio. By then it was nearly seven, and Vicky had purposely left waking her before then.

At Vicky's entry she had given her an apologetic smile. 'I feel a fraud,' she said. 'I don't think I've had a lie-in since I spent a week with my sister, five years ago. I didn't really enjoy it then. I'm so used to being up and about.'

'Ross went out at six,' Vicky said, as she placed the tray by the bedside. 'Does he usually get himself something before he goes?' she asked.

'Don't worry about that,' Mrs George assured her. 'All he has is a cup of tea, and he can get that for himself. It won't hurt him for once.'

Which meant that Mrs George did get it for him, Vicky thought, but as things stood, she heartily agreed with Mrs George's comments that he could look after himself. It was bad enough anticipating the row that was looming up in front of her at breakfast when he was due to put in an appearance, without having to be shouted at before she was properly awake!

At nine o'clock, Vicky waited until she heard Ross pull up outside the homestead, and hastily putting his breakfast on a hot plate and leaving it to keep warm, made a hasty retreat back to her room, ostensibly to make her bed—at least that was her excuse, but any other would have done.

She might have known she wouldn't get away with it. 'Victoria!' Ross's voice thundered up the stairs towards her, and caused her eyebrows to lift. She had not been called 'Victoria' for years, not since Mrs Janson departed from the scene, for she was the only one who had insisted on calling her by her name and not an abbreviated version.

Since she knew it was no good pretending she had not heard the imperious summons, Vicky went

down to join him wishing that she felt as brave as
she was trying to pretend she was.

He was just finishing his breakfast, and was in
the act of making himself some coffee, and he
pointed with an autocratic finger towards the other
seat at the kitchen table, then turned back to his task
again, taking it for granted that she would obey.

Having no choice in the matter, Vicky sat and
waited for the storm to descend upon her.

Ross strode back to the table with his coffee,
and Vicky took particular notice of the fact that he
had not asked if she would like a cup, but then she
was up for the jump, and couldn't expect solicitous
treatment.

'Enjoy yourself last night?' he shot out at her as
he sat down.

Vicky looked back at him, highly resenting
having to account for her movements, but her
indignation vanished as she saw a dark bruise
under Ross's left eye. He had been in a fight, and
she did not need to be told who his opponent had
been.

Seeing her expression as her eyes lingered on the
bruise, he nodded grimly. 'I warned him to keep
away from you,' he said quietly, 'but he chose to
ignore it. You won't be getting any invitations from
that quarter again,' he added complacently.

'I think that I shall go and see how Pete is,' she
ground out, her earlier dismay over the fight now
turning to concern over Pete, 'and apologise for
what happened to him,' she added furiously, considering that he had acted like a gentleman with

her, not once stepping out of line, and this was his reward!

'You'll do no such thing!' Ross shouted at her. 'I'll lock you in your room first! You'll let things be. You've caused me enough trouble. From now on you'll do just what you're told to do. I meant it when I said I'd give you a tanning, and it's what you'll get if you disobey me,' he added harshly.

Judging by the dangerous glints in his eyes, Vicky was sure it would not take much for him to dish out that treatment right then and there, but she was furious herself, and her brown eyes held tawny glints in them as she shouted back at him, 'You lay one hand on me, Ross Janson, and I'll walk out of this station. It's just a job to me, and you're my employer—that's how I see it, but it doesn't give you the right to tell me what to do in my spare time. It's all your fault anyway,' she added, goaded beyond discretion. 'If you hadn't given me such enlightening lessons on flirting I wouldn't have accepted a date from Pete.' Her eyes flashed out at him. 'I just wanted to see if he measured up to your standards!'

Ross's blue eyes widened in shock for a second, then a blaze of fury swept through them. 'And did he?' he asked in a menacingly soft voice.

Vicky ought to have recognised the danger signals, but she was too far gone to acknowledge them, she only knew that she wanted to hit out at him. 'Oh, yes,' she replied sweetly, 'a little better, if anything,' she added for good measure.

Ross leant towards her and gave her a hard

stinging slap across the cheek, and she stared back
at him in disbelief. No one had ever slapped her
like that before, not even when she was a child,
and her hand, that went up to the still stinging
area, trembled. She knew a sense of shock that
went deeper than outrage, if she had had any
doubts about the way Ross felt about her, she had
received confirmation from that one action of his,
and the look of disdain in his eyes as he calmly
watched her reaction to his swift punishment.
'That,' Ross said grimly, 'is just for starters. It
might teach you to watch your words. Pete Noonan
might be a ladies' man, but he knows where to
draw the line. He'd have more sense than to tangle
with a kid like you for a start. If I thought otherwise, he'd have more than a sore jaw to complain
of. He wanted to rile me—well, he succeeded, and
that's all there is to it. I told you before how it
was, so don't go making up fairy tales, because
nobody will believe you,' he added harshly.

Vicky drew in a quick sobbing breath. It was
one thing being on the receiving end of physical
punishment, but quite another listening to someone
telling you that you were a liar, and what was
worse, being told that you weren't attractive
enough to receive overtures from any man! All
right, so she had embellished a little, but Pete had
kissed her, and he hadn't had to, but this cocksure
man wouldn't believe it. 'Thank you,' she said
quietly, 'for showing me what you're really like.
Just a big bully who intends to get his own way no
matter what.' Her voice trembled as she went on,

'Did it ever occur to you that I might really like Pete Noonan? Of course not!' she exclaimed bitterly. 'Such a thought never entered your head, did it? You're too sure of yourself, that's your trouble. Everything's been easy for you, hasn't it? You can't bear to lose, can you? Even when it concerns someone like me who's just a kid in your estimation. Well, for your information, Pete didn't see me like that. He treated me as a woman ought to be treated. I don't think he found me unattractive—if he did, he was too kind to show the fact.' Her voice shook. 'Even if I don't see him again, I shall always be grateful for that,' she got out.

She walked to the door. If she didn't get out of there right away, she would break down, and that was the last thing she wanted. She drew a deep breath. 'For Mrs George's sake, I shall stay until she's on her feet again, but don't you ever dare touch me again—in fact, the less I see of you, the better!' she added coldly, and made her exit with her head proudly erect.

That's telling him, she thought wildly, as she made her way to her room, feeling oddly proud of herself for making a stand and not letting her emotions get the better of her and reduce her to a weeping wreck, but it had been a close thing.

A few moments after she had reached her room, she heard Ross's Land Rover start up, and with a roar of the engine, he was off.

Vicky sat down weakly on her half-made bed. Everything was going wrong. It was as if the fates had decided to line up against her. No matter what

she tried, it backfired on her, and all she had
wanted to do was to free Ross and herself from an
old understanding. Considering their tempera-
ments it shouldn't have been all that hard, but she
hadn't allowed for Ross's stubborn pride. He didn't
have to go and knock Pete down. If he had used
his head, he would have seen that she had given
him an excellent opportunity to back out of the
arrangement without being made to look a heel, as
Mary had put it that day.

Her hand went up to feel the cheek that he had
slapped so hard. It was still sore, and as she glanced
across at the dressing-table mirror in front of her,
she saw that there was a red mark where the impact
had been. 'That's for starters,' had been what he'd
said afterwards, she thought, and he had meant it.
She had read about battered wives, but not
battered fiancées. Not that they were still engaged,
and even the few unenlightened ones would soon
be aware of that fact, if they didn't know now, she
thought, thinking of the hot line that was sure to
be buzzing with the news.

She got up quickly as she felt hot tears stinging
her eyes. She was not going to cry over a man like
that, she told herself as she straightened her slim
shoulders. What a blessing in disguise her visit to
Jarra had been! She might never have known the
other side of Ross Janson's character, that he was
an implacable, overbearing, autocratic, dictator-
ial—she ran out of expletives, and took a deep
breath. How could anyone love a man like that?
Ella Waden was welcome to him! And she only

hoped that she could stand up for herself!

Sick of her own company and the gloom now descending upon her, Vicky went to see Mrs George, who welcomed her with one of her rare smiles, and Vicky thought how nice it was to receive such a welcome, even though Mrs George was in the enemy camp, and she longed to get back to Dale's Creek and the quiet calming presence of Mary.

If Mrs George had heard anything on the open lines about Vicky's defection from Ross to Pete Noonan, she said nothing of it. She seemed genuinely pleased to have Vicky's company, and pointed to a chair opposite hers for Vicky to make herself comfortable.

The housekeeper's quarters were of ample proportions, and well furnished, forming a self-contained suite, consisting of sitting-room, dining-room, bedroom and bathroom. It was useful for keeping in the background when there were guests in the house, and had been Mrs Janson's idea of giving her staff privacy, and providing the same for her family.

With Mrs George working on her tapestry work, and Vicky trying to push all thoughts of her brush with Ross out of her mind, they settled down to a cosy chat.

Of all the subjects they might have discussed Vicky had not expected to find herself listening to Mrs George going back in time when the Waden family and the Jansons and Dales were a closer knit community. It all started when Mrs George told her how Ella had once been a frequent caller, and how she hadn't seen much of her for the past year or so.

'I think Ella's had a rough deal,' she confided in Vicky. 'Being pretty isn't everything, and she's the kind of girl who needs company. Losing her mother at that early age—let me see—she was about seven, I think, when her mother died. I'm not saying that her father didn't make a good job of bringing her up, but he doesn't seem to realise that she has her own life to lead,' she sighed. 'Not that she's ever complained, but everybody knows how it is.'

Vicky wondered at this point if Mrs George was trying to tell her something about Ross and Ella, in which case she did know about Vicky and Pete, and was probably preparing Vicky for future events.

'Her father,' Mrs George went on, 'meant well. Of course he wanted his daughter to make a good marriage, everyone does, but unless Ella married one of the directors of the consortium, which wasn't likely—they're all rather elderly, you know—I think he was asking too much of her. She could have gone to live with an aunt in Sydney, but her father would not hear of it.' She handed Vicky her embroidery bag and said, 'See if you can find me some more of this blue, dear, please,' and went back to the Wadens. 'There was a time when Mr Janson was considering taking over Albury, or the Waden station as it was then,' she said musingly. 'It was in a pretty poor state then, and

Mr Waden hadn't a hope of keeping it going when he inherited it from his father. He'd no capital, you see.'

She nodded at the silk skein of blue that Vicky handed her. 'Thank you, dear. Now where was I? Oh, yes, I think Ross's father would have taken it over if it hadn't been for Mrs Janson. She and Mrs Waden simply didn't get on. No, that's not quite right,' she corrected herself as she threaded the silk through her needle. 'Mrs Waden put herself out to get an entrée into Mrs Janson's set. Mrs Janson wasn't a snob, at least, not really a snob, but she did set a lot on what she considered good class, and Mrs Waden was a pushing sort of woman. She had looks, but not much sense, you know, and no tact at all, and certainly had an eye for the future. In fact, she was everything that Mrs Janson disliked in a woman. If Mr Janson had taken over the station he would have left Mr Waden as manager, he couldn't have done anything else, and that would have meant a closer association between them, which was something that Mrs Janson definitely did not want.' She smiled at Vicky. 'So they looked towards Dale's Creek for the expansion they felt would be needed in a few years' time.'

Not only expansion, thought Vicky, but a bride for Ross as well. If Mrs Janson had not taken a dislike to Ella's mother, Ella would have been Mrs Janson's choice for him, since she could have had no objection to Ella, who would certainly have made the kind of daughter-in-law that she had wanted.

She wondered why Ella had not been to see Mrs George for such a long time. Was it because it was becoming too hard for her to face up to the fact that Ross would shortly be marrying someone else? Her mind went back to the party. She could not recall any special look between them that told of their affection for each other—but then, she thought sadly, they were both past the stage where their emotions might let them down. They had learned to live with it for so long that it was natural to keep their feelings on a tight rein. Just as it was natural for Ross to assume that she, Vicky, did not know her own mind. He thought of her as a wilful child having tantrums that he didn't intend her to get away with. She had to be taught how to conform, and if she married him, life would be one hard lesson after another, simply because she did not see things the same way as he did.

All these thoughts went through her mind while she listened to Mrs George recounting tales of the past, one part of her attentive, the other wandered off into her own reverie.

After that morning's encounter with Ross, Vicky had no intention of an encore. She had said all that she was going to say, and knew that it would be a long time before Ross forgave her—if he ever did, that was. In any case she wasn't hanging around to find out.

When the meal was ready, she served up Mrs George's portion, and then Ross's, which she placed in the oven warmer for him, leaving his

place set on the kitchen table, and then took up
Mrs George's tray, hearing the Land Rover drawing up as she started up the stairs and automatically
quickening her steps to avoid meeting him as he
came in the door.

Ross would think that she had taken her meal
with Mrs George, and Mrs George would think
that she was eating with Ross, and that left her at
least an hour of peace in her room until she could
go down to do the dishes, by which time Ross
should have retired to his study to catch up with
some paper work, since that, she had learned from
Mrs George, was the usual routine at Jarra. As for
the latter part of the evening, Vicky intended to
spend it with Mrs George, and if not, then in her
room. Whatever happened, she meant to keep her
word and stay out of Ross's proximity. Her brushes
with him always left her feeling like the Ugly
Duckling, only she wasn't going to turn into a
swan, not in his eyes or anybody else's, not that
she wanted to be anybody else but who she was,
but it made good sense to keep her distance while
she still had a shred of confidence in herself!

The following morning brought a visitor to
Jarra, and Vicky, preparing the mid-morning coffee
for herself and Mrs George, heard a car drawing
up in front of the homestead and slipped through
to the lounge to see who their visitor was. Her eyes
widened in surprise when she saw Ella Waden
alighting with a basket in her hand, and going back
to the kitchen Vicky reached for another cup and
saucer.

A second later Ella came into the kitchen with the basket of fruit. 'I thought Mrs George might appreciate some peaches,' she said to Vicky. 'Rotten luck falling like that,' she added, in a flat voice.

Vicky gave her a quick glance before she put two cups and saucers on a tray. There had been no smile of welcome from Ella, in fact, Vicky thought, it was not unlike her welcome at Albury the other night, and gave her the distinct feeling that her visit was not altogether an altruistic one. Ella had something on her mind, and she was not pleased with Vicky, that much was certain, and Vicky was in no mood for yet another lecture on what was considered her bad taste in consorting with Pete Noonan. 'I was just going to take Mrs George's coffee up,' she said lightly, picking the tray up and starting to walk to the door, giving Ella no choice but to follow her. 'She'll be pleased to see you,' she added firmly, and led the way up to her room.

Mrs George was pleased to see her visitor, and accepted the fruit with open pleasure, and began to relate how she had had the accident, with Ella listening sympathetically, and half apologising for not calling before now, but offered no excuse for her absence from the scene, except mentioning vaguely that she was doing some work in the office line for the consortium and had been frightfully busy for weeks.

Vicky edged near the door while she was talking, meaning to make her escape and leave them alone to have a chat, when Mrs George, seeing that there were only two cups of coffee on the tray, exclaimed, 'We'll need another cup, Vicky,' and at Vicky's excuse that she had a few things to do, replied, 'Nonsense! Nothing that can't wait, I know. You go and get another cup.'

Vicky had no option but to comply with this direction, and returned to the kitchen to collect her coffee, not looking forward to the cosy chat Mrs George obviously anticipated.

Ross's name inevitably cropped up in the conversation, and Vicky sensed rather than saw Ella glance her way. It was on Ross's account that she was angry with her, she thought, and that settled it for Vicky. Ella was in love with Ross, it was the only answer. Instead of being in the clouds at Ross's freedom, for surely she could see a happy ending at last, she was absolutely furious with Vicky. No one, thought Vicky, was reacting the way they should have done, and it was all rather odd.

After a little further thought on this, Vicky began to see how it was for Ella. To have been in love with someone for years, only to find that the person in the way of your happiness had turned out to be a silly chit of a girl who had become embroiled with such a man as Pete Noonan, must have been galling, to put it mildly, she mused silently. It must seem like wasted years to the unhappy Ella.

When the visit drew to a close, Vicky gave an inward sigh of relief which was shortlived, for when Ella got up to go, she asked if Vicky could find a plate for the peaches as she needed the basket, and handing Vicky the coffee tray gave her no option but to accompany her downstairs, in spite of Mrs George's suggestion that they use a very pretty fruit dish that she possessed, and that Vicky would find in her dining-room cabinet, a suggestion that Ella chose not to hear, for she was already at the door of the sitting-room and expecting Vicky to follow her.

Once in the realms of the kitchen and out of earshot of Mrs George, Ella rounded on Vicky, hardly giving her time to put the coffee tray down. 'Keep away from Pete Noonan,' she said in a hard tight voice. 'You've got a perfectly good man of your own. Stick to your own territory,' she advised her grimly.

Vicky's brow shot up, and a surge of anger swept through her. She was sick of receiving advice from all and sundry! What business was it of Ella's? She was as bad as Ross! Her eyes met Ella's grim ones. 'And if I choose not to?' she said coldly.

Ella banged the basket that Vicky had just handed her down on the kitchen table, and Vicky got the distinct impression that she wished it was her head. 'Look,' Ella said caustically, 'Pete had his own reasons for dating you. I'm telling you to keep away from him for your own good. You'll only make a colossal fool of yourself if you don't.'

Vicky felt like shaking her head. Was Ella warning her for her own benefit—or was there more to it? Had Ross asked her to have a word with her? Or was it Mr Waden who had sent her out on the mission? It was a more likely solution that he had.

Perhaps he felt responsible as Pete was on his pay-roll.

As Vicky had no intention of seeing Pete again, she decided to set Ella's mind at rest, although she did not look worried, furious, yes, but definitely not worried.

'I suppose your father sent you?' Vicky said quietly. 'Well, you can tell him there's nothing to worry about. It's a storm in a teacup, as they say,' she added sardonically.

Ella stared at her and then gave a dry chuckle that held no amusement in it. 'That's good,' she said in a hard voice. 'Father wouldn't lift a finger to stop you seeing Pete. In fact, he'd encourage you.'

It was Vicky's turn to stare. 'I don't get this,' she said bewilderedly. 'What does it matter to you——' she blinked, as a thought struck her. It couldn't be that Ella——? 'You and Pete?' she asked with a note of incredulity in her voice.

Ella's eyes met Vicky's wide eyes and then dropped hastily to the table. 'Yes,' she said quietly.

Vicky heard her answer but was having difficulty in believing it. Yet it all made sense. It explained why Ella had never married. She looked at the other girl. 'Your father?' she began.

'Knows nothing about it,' Ella cut in bitterly. 'Pete would be shot off Albury at a moment's notice if he knew.'

Vicky could well believe it. 'Was that why Pete——' she began, sorting out her thoughts as she went along.

Ella again interrupted her. 'Sheer frustration,' she said, 'and to try and get me to make my mind up about marrying him. We'd have to go away, of course. Pete would lose his job, and we'd have nowhere to go either,' she ended miserably. 'Neither of us has any money.'

Vicky felt a spurt of sympathy for Ella. She had felt sorry for her before when she had thought that she was in love with Ross, but her predicament was apparently ten times worse than that. She had fallen in love with the wrong person—wrong, that was, from her father's viewpoint, and Vicky could see little hope of a happy ending.

'That's why Pete took a sudden shine to you,' Ella said in a dull voice. 'We'd had a fight, and he was punishing me by making a dead set at you. Oh, I was jealous enough. I could have scratched your eyes out at that party. And when he had the gall to bring you up to Albury——' Her voice faltered.

Vicky touched her arm in a reassuring way. 'He acted the perfect gentleman, Ella,' she said soothingly, deciding not to mention the kiss he had given her. It had only been a token gesture anyway. 'I thought he was having a go at Ross, and that was why he picked on me,' she said with a smile. 'Otherwise, it didn't make sense. I'm nothing to write home about, am I? So there had to be a reason.'

'Oh—I didn't mean——' Ella began hastily.

'Oh, yes you did,' Vicky replied, still smiling. 'And you're right. I was having my own private fight with Ross at the time—still am, if it comes to that, so I didn't mind falling in with Pete's plans—only I wouldn't have done, if I'd known about you,' she reassured Ella. 'You see, I thought I was helping you—I thought you and Ross——' she grinned at Ella's startled look, 'well, he did have a crush on you once, didn't he?'

'Oh, that was years ago,' Ella replied lightly. 'He got tired long before I did. I used to dream about him,' she added with a wistful smile, then her face sobered. 'Then there was Pete.' She was silent for a moment. 'I know what everyone says about him. But he's not like that now. He used to play around. He's too good-looking for his own good, that's his trouble. Women made fools of themselves over him, and he encouraged it. But he's through with all that now. I think at first he tried to date me as a kind of dare he'd had with himself, to see if he could get me to fall for him, and I ignored him, and that made him pretty mad. It also sobered him up and made him think a little more seriously about the future.' She gave a wistful smile. 'He knows there's no future at Albury for him, not if we marry, but he says he'll get something somewhere, if I say yes.'

Her hands clenched round the handle of the basket. 'But it's not that easy. I know he wants to make sure of me, and he's afraid——' she hesitated and looked back at Vicky. 'He knows Father's hoping——' she met Vicky's interested eyes, 'well, we all expected Ross to announce your wedding plans at the party, and when he didn't, it started

everyone wondering—I mean, he has taken over
Dale's Creek, hasn't he?' She took a deep breath.
'It certainly started Father thinking, anyway. He's
always believed that if it hadn't been for that
arrangement between your parents Ross would
have chosen me. Fathers are like that, you know,'
she ended sardonically.

Vicky nodded understandingly. 'What are you
going to do, Ella?' she asked quietly.

Ella drew in a quick breath. 'Say yes to Pete,'
she said quietly, 'before Ross really goes to town
on him. Pete's no fighter, and Ross knows how to
use his fists. I'm worried that Dad might get to
hear of the fight. It's Ross's side that he'll take, of
course, for obvious reasons. He won't fire Pete,
but he'll send him to one of the outstations and I'll
never see him. It's difficult enough as it is.' She ran
a hand over the handles of the basket. 'I sneak out
to see him twice a week on the excuse that I'm
visiting Mrs George. He's no objection to that, and
he's never queried it.'

She looked up at Vicky. 'If it came to the push,
I don't think Mrs George would let me down.
She doesn't know that I'm using her as an alibi,
but I'm sure she'll understand when she knows the
truth, she knows I wouldn't do anything really
wrong, and she knows how it is with Father,' she
said lamely, adding tiredly, 'but he's not stupid. I
think he knows there is someone, but doesn't know
who.' She gave Vicky a wry grin. 'When Pete took
a sudden shine to you, I guess it took some of the
suspicion off Pete, although I don't think he

seriously considered him as a threat.'

Vicky understood this too. She had thought the same. Ella was too level-headed to fall in love with a womaniser, or someone who had once been a womaniser, even if they had now mended their ways. Vicky wished she could do something to help Ella, but didn't see what. Ella wanted Ross to keep away from Pete, and he would only do that if Vicky kept her distance from Pete. Ella had known that, of course, hence her warning to Vicky earlier. 'I wish there was something I could do,' she said to Ella.

Ella gave her a smile. 'Thanks anyway,' she replied lightly, and gave a shrug. 'I guess it's in the hands of fate now. I'm burning my boats. I only know that I love Pete and that he loves me. We'll just have to take off. Father will have to come to terms with it one day, I know that there's no way that he'll accept it now, so we've no option but to run for it.' She gave a slight moue. 'I just wanted to make sure that Pete was fit for travel at a moment's notice,' she said at an attempt at raillery, and picked the basket up. 'Thanks for the coffee and sympathy,' she said, as she walked to the door and paused as she reached it. 'I guess you've your own troubles, huh? Ross is a fine man, Vicky. If it wasn't for Pete, then I'd give you some opposition, not that I think I'd be successful, mind you. He seems to have a one-track mind where you're concerned——' She hesitated. 'I can trust you, can't I, Vicky? not to mention——?

Vicky nodded quickly. 'Of course you can,' she said reassuringly. The next minute Ella had gone.

CHAPTER NINE

VICKY stood gazing at the dust clouds in the wake of Ella's car's departure. Her mind was full of the news of Ella and Pete. If the news came as a shock to her, she could well imagine Mr Waden's reaction. In the local idiom, he would 'go bananas'!

She went over what Ella had said about Ross being a fine man. Of course he was a fine man, but he wasn't her man, she thought crossly, and wondered why no one bothered to wonder if she was in love with him, or if he was in love with her, and he wasn't, and she wasn't—oh, dear, she thought, what a muddle it all was!

At least Ella and Pete upheld the good old tradition of romance. Ella loved Pete and Pete loved Ella, and goodness knew what sacrifices they would have to make to stay together. They had no money, but were prepared to risk everything on the cause of true love. Vicky sighed. They say that fortune favours the brave, she thought, and she hoped that in his case it proved true.

She was so busy with her thoughts that she did not notice the time, and it was only when she heard Ross's Land Rover draw up in front of the homestead that she realised that he was back for lunch, and she had to make a dash to get a salad for him,

thanking providence that there was a dish already
prepared in the fridge, and all she had to do was to
cut up some cold meat to go with it, and with any
luck she could get it done before he came down
from the quick shower he usually took before sitting down to lunch.

She almost made it, but whether Ross had
guessed her intention of doing the disappearing act
before his appearance, he was certainly quick off
the mark, for they met at the kitchen door, and
Vicky would have gone past him had he not caught
her by the arm. 'Do you have to be so childish?' he
said furiously. 'Okay, so I was rough on you the
other day, but it was only for your own good.'

Vicky's brows lifted. He had actually apologised!
At least, that was as near as he would get to an
apology, she thought darkly.

'Look,' said Ross, running an impatient hand
through his dark hair, 'did you really mean what
you said about liking Pete Noonan?' he asked
quietly.

Vicky's eyes rested on the tiled floor. She knew
what it had cost him to ask that question. He had
his pride. 'Yes,' she said slowly. It was not a lie,
she did like Pete, and she was liking him a lot more
than she was liking Ross at that particular time.

Ross's thoughtful, 'I see,' somewhat surprised
her, and she looked up at him, but he was not
looking at her, but focusing his attention ahead of
him. That was all he said, but Vicky knew with
certainty that he had accepted her word. Without
any further discussion, she knew that he would

leave Pete alone. She also knew something else. She was free, it was as if he had told her that he would not stand in her way, that he had accepted her decision to go her own way.

Vicky went up to her room in a thoughtful mood. She ought to be brimming with success, but she felt very let down. She had felt like this before, and there was no accounting for it. Nothing she could put her finger on, so what on earth was the matter with her? Why was it that whenever Ross behaved in a rational and perfectly normal way, she was made to feel wretched?

The answer came as she closed her bedroom door behind her. It had closed with a final snap, she was this side, and Ross was on the other side of the door, shut out because she had wanted it that way. She thought of his strong arms around her, and the kiss he had given her. This awakened memories of Pete and the quick kiss he had given her, and of the way she had felt at the light contact of a stranger's lips. It had repelled her, that was the only way she could put it, because—Her eyes opened wide. Oh, no—not that! She hadn't fallen in love with Ross, had she?

She walked over to her bed and sat down weakly. She had! Of all the dumb, foolish, impossible things to do! She had done precisely what everyone expected her to do, Ross included! Which was fine, she thought bitterly, except for the fact that Ross did not love her!

Vicky counted off the days before she could leave Jarra. Four days at least, she thought miserably,

and somehow she had to act like her old self, and
not give the show away. Ross knew her a little too
well for her liking. She had no excuse now for
keeping out of his way, and would be expected to
have dinner with him. She remembered the way he
had spotted her surreptitious survey of him the last
time she had had dinner with him, and she groaned
inwardly. What on earth was she going to do?

Her slim shoulders straightened. She would act
normally, she told herself sternly. Nothing really
had changed. She was still in the same position she
had been in before. She shook her head slowly, no,
that was not true. Everything had changed for her.
She hadn't had any breaks at all. If Mrs George
had not fallen and sprained her ankle, she would
not have come to Jarra. Would not have realised
that she did love Ross, and must have loved him
all the time. It had only taken a shaking up to
realise it.

Her chin lifted. Ross had his pride, and she had
hers. Her pride would not allow him to marry her.
Not when she knew the way he felt about her. To
him, she was just Vicky, the little girl next door
and to whom he felt an obligation.

The following week passed slowly for Vicky. Mrs
George was pronounced fit five days after Vicky's
last encounter with Ross. Had she but known it,
her worry of giving the game away during the
evening dinner sessions she had thought she would
be having with Ross turned out to be groundless,
for Ross was not present. He appeared to have
other engagements, a meeting here, and a meeting

there, and it all sounded perfectly reasonable. Mrs George, for one, did not show any surprise at his absence from the scene and even half apologised to Vicky for his absorption in farming matters. 'Being president of the local farming community places a lot of responsibility on his shoulders,' she explained. 'It means a lot of evening work for him, particularly at this time of year.'

Although Vicky agreed with everything that Mrs George had said, for she knew full well how busy Ross had been in the past, she could not rid herself of a suspicion that his absence was a deliberate ploy on his part to keep out of her way. She also suspected that having washed his hands of her, he was making sure that he was not around to provide a shoulder for her to weep on when the crash came—in other words, when Pete Noonan got tired of the game.

When at last Vicky was able to return to Dale's Creek, she knew a feeling of relief mingled with sadness, for she was not only leaving Jarra, but the man she loved, and there had been times when her emotions had got the better of her good sense and she had wanted to wait up for Ross to return from his meetings and fling herself at him, telling him that she had made a ghastly mistake, and that he was the only one for her and could they please get married.

In these dreamy imaginings she would conveniently forget all her previous good resolutions of giving Ross a chance to choose his own bride. Nothing mattered but that she should have him by her side for the rest of time.

Now, as she motored back to Dale's Creek; she was grateful that she had confined these fond imaginings to the world of dreams and had not given way to temptation. She even felt a little proud of herself for standing firm. If Ross had truly loved her, he would have fought for her, instead of making a half-hearted effort to keep her away from Pete, and that had been through pride and not any other reason.

Mary's welcoming smile and 'Hi!' as she walked into the homestead brought a film of tears to her eyes, and she hastily passed through the hall and on up to her room, after returning her greeting with what she hoped sounded as cheery as Mary's greeting.

When she got to her room, she took a deep breath. She would have to get a hold of herself. She was acting like a stupid schoolgirl with her first crush, she told herself scathingly. How right Ross had been over that, she thought. She had not grown up at all.

As she threw her case on to her bed, she shook her head. She had grown up, but the transformation had come too suddenly for her to cope with, she thought wearily, and she would not confide in anyone, least of all Mary, who would understand only too well, and would protect her from any further heartbreak, and sympathy was something that Vicky could not take at that time. Mary would probably guess in time, but until Vicky was able to handle the situation her way, she had to keep her from finding out, and goodness knew how she was going to do that. Look at the way she had reacted to Mary's smiling welcome just now, she thought sadly. Another minute and she would have been howling her eyes out, pouring it all out to Mary, and that would never do.

There was her father too, she thought with a wild jerk of panic. If he were to discover what a mess she had made of things, he would try to put things right for her. He would tell Ross that she loved him, of that she had no doubt, and she would be back to square one with a vengeance, let alone the embarrassment such a situation would put her in.

With such thoughts on her mind, Vicky dreaded the next few days when she would have to attempt to return to the normal routine of life back at Dale's Creek. On the whole she managed well enough, although she had felt Mary giving her a few hard looks now and again, and wondered if she had overdone her heartiness at being back home again, particularly as she was so forthcoming when normally she was on the quiet side.

Her father, however, saw nothing unusual in her behaviour, and for that she was grateful. He was, it appeared, thoroughly happy with his situation, and although the job Ross had offered him had sounded a menial one to Vicky, from all accounts it suited him, and the fact that Ross had also offered him the post of secretary to the farming community of which he was the president had given a definite fillip to his confidence, and the talk was

mostly confined to policies made at the meetings
he now attended with Ross.

With Jake and Mary for company, let alone the
good food provided by Mary, and the odd hand of
cards with Jake, Gordon Dale's life was happier
than it had been for some time, and that should
have made Vicky content too. What had once been
a shell of a homestead, with two lonely people in-
habiting it, had now become once more a real
home, and if it were not for the twinges of heart-
ache Vicky felt, her life would have been happier
too. As it was, she found herself listening for news
of Ross, and what he was up to, and these were
provided by her father, and what Ross had said at
a particular meeting, and how much he was looked
up to by his fellow members of the community.

So the days passed, and all Vicky had to do was
to keep a firm rein on her emotions. The danger
points came when she was alone with Mary and
they indulged in local gossip.

Mary had never asked her about Pete Noonan,
and Vicky, although a little surprised, did not bring
the subject up either. It was a little too near other
subjects she had no wish to discuss with Mary.

A fortnight after Vicky had returned home, and
when things had settled down and she began to
think that it might be possible for her to look forward to the future—a future that did not involve
the man she loved, but the quiet acceptance of the
fact that she was not the only one who had suffered
the fate of unrequited love, and would certainly
not be the last, a telephone call from Albury started

a train of events that jerked her out of her fatalistic musings.

It began with Mrs Richards, the Albury house-keeper, asking to speak to Ross, and Vicky, taking the initial call, handed over to her father who had just come in and who would know where Ross was. She heard her father say that he would get a message sent down to him as he was in the lower paddocks. Hearing this, Vicky made a quick retreat in case she was asked to find Ross. She knew he had made several visits since her return home, but she had made a point of avoiding coming into contact with him. This was not hard to do. He rarely came to the homestead, but spent his time on the station inspecting the stock and giving orders for improving the running of the station.

In the normal run of events Vicky would be bound to run into him at some time during these visits, for in the past she had never confined herself to the boundaries of the homestead, but had borrowed one of the station hands' mounts for her excursions over the station. Now, however, her activities had been cut down simply because of the fear of meeting Ross. She too had her pride, and the more she had thought about her last few days at Jarra, the more convinced she was that Ross had deliberately gone out of his way to avoid her company, in spite of what Mrs George had said.

When Ross arrived at the homestead, Vicky was in the kitchen with Mary, helping to prepare the vegetables for lunch. The sound of his car pulling up outside the homestead was clearly heard by both of them. 'That sounds like Ross's motor,' said Mary, as she put the vegetables on to boil. 'Is he coming to lunch?' she asked Vicky.

Vicky then told her about the phone call from Albury and that she doubted that he would be staying for lunch, hoping that no such offer was made, in case he accepted!

'Mr Waden's away, isn't he?' Mary mused, as she turned the heat down under the pans now boiling merrily. 'I expect something's cropped up and they need some advice.'

As Vicky got the plates out of the kitchen cupboard a thought suddenly struck her, and she stared unseeingly at the Willow Pattern plates in her hand. She had a good idea of what had 'cropped up'. 'Where is Mr Waden?' she asked.

'At a conference up north—at least, he's on his way. Won't get there until tomorrow,' Mary replied, starting to lay the table.

Vicky put the plates ready for the dishing up of the meal and moved towards the door that led out to the hall. Ella had eloped with Pete! She was sure of it! What better chance would they have? she thought. With Ella's father so far away they would have a good head start on any attempt at pursuit.

From her hovering position by the hallway door, Vicky could hear Ross on the telephone, but could not be seen. Mary was too busy with the lunch to notice her blatant eavesdropping.

For a moment Vicky thought she had missed hearing the information she wanted, but Ross must have been listening to what Mrs Richard was telling him, then she heard him say, 'When?' and this was followed by a harsh-sounding, 'Are you sure?' and then, 'I'm coming over,' and the hard click of the receiver being put down. 'Going over to Albury,' Ross called out to Mr Dale. 'Get Jake to get on with the clearing out of that scrub land we were looking at,' he said, and marched out of the homestead.

Vicky knew a sense of disappointment. Ross had said nothing about the reason why he was going to Albury, and she wondered if she had been wrong in assuming that Ella had left with Pete, but she could see no other reason for Ross's reticence. If the whole thing turned out to be a mare's nest, then the less said about it the better. It was not a thing the Wadens would want broadcast.

On the other hand, she mused, if it was true, then the news would spread like wildfire round the district and nothing Ross could do would prevent it becoming known.

'Wonder what all that was about,' Vicky's father commented at lunch. 'Mrs Richards was in a right tizzy, and that's not like her,' he added musingly. 'Not like Ross not to put us in the picture either,' he added, then sat up straight as a thought struck him. 'Say, you don't think there's a scare on, do you?' he asked Jake.

Jake finished the last of his meal, and shaking his head at Mary's offer of a second helping, commented, 'I doubt it. If it is, we'll know in good time. Ross isn't one to hang about.'

An hour later Vicky got the news she was waiting

for. Ross rang her father, and hearing the ring of the telephone she moved the chair that she had taken out on to the porch a little nearer the office window so that she would hear what was said.

Her father's surprised, 'Well, I'm danged!' was the first proof, and his, 'George will be fit to be tied!' comment settled the matter for Vicky, as she quietly replaced her chair back against the door of the homestead and settled down again in the sunshine.

Good for Ella and Pete, she thought drowsily, and she wished them bon voyage. Whatever happened now, they would be together. Even if Ella's father did find them, they would have to marry, because it would be several days before he could get home and however much he hated it, he would have to accept Pete as his son-in-law, for the sake of Ella if nothing else.

A few minutes later Mary joined her on the porch, and Vicky's father came out bursting with the news. 'Say, what do you think? Ella Waden's lit out with Pete Noonan!'

Vicky saw Mary glance at her before asking, 'Is that true?' in a shocked voice.

'Ross says so,' replied Gordon Dale, 'and Ross doesn't spread rumours, does he? It's true all right!' He shook his head. 'Ella must have got sunstroke,' he said, 'there's no accounting otherwise for her doing a thing like that—not with someone like Noonan. She's got a mite too much sense for that.'

Vicky felt an urge to stand up for Pete, but wisely held her tongue. The less she said, the better, she thought.

'Ross found someone who thinks he knows where they're heading,' Mr Dale continued. 'Seems he's been receiving mail from Mildura, and he's taken off after them. With any luck he'll catch them up before they reach the highway. They're travelling in Noonan's old roadster, and she'll only do about thirty on good roads. Seems they left around seven—Mrs Richards thinks she heard a car's engine at the back of the homestead. That was before she saw the note Ella had left propped up on the mantelpiece for her father to find when he got home.'

Vicky was so indignant at Ross's interference, she had spoken before she had time to think. 'Why should Ross take that on?' she demanded crossly. 'It's Ella's father's job to go after them.'

'Seeing as George is up the North, it's up to Ross to do something about it,' replied her father. 'It's what he would be expected to do. I offered to go myself, but Ross wouldn't hear of it. I wouldn't care to be in Noonan's shoes when he does catch them up,' he added with a chuckle. 'Ross sounded set to give him a right thrashing!'

When Vicky's father had left the room to go in search of Jake and tell him the news, Vicky, meeting Mary's eyes, was surprised to find a look of sympathy in them. 'That doesn't sound like Ross,' Mary said quietly. 'Ella's old enough to know what she's doing.'

Vicky said nothing. She was not supposed to know anything about it, and did not intend to get caught up in the coming backlash of Ella's father's temper when he heard the news.

The look of sympathy in Mary's eyes as she had looked at her after she had heard the news still puzzled her, and her mind was busy finding the explanation. Then she had it. Mary must think that she had fallen for Pete! Perhaps Ross had said something, asking for Mary's co-operation perhaps in watching out for Vicky's interests?

Mary picked up her knitting and shook her head sadly. 'So it was Ella after all, wasn't it?' she said slowly.

Vicky blinked, then frowned, and seeing her puzzlement Mary went on, 'I can't see Ross interfering like that unless he had a very good reason, can you?' she said. 'It's not as if Ella was a flighty young girl. She knows what she's doing all right.'

It took a minute or so for Vicky to get her meaning, and she drew in her breath sharply. Ross loved Ella! He intended to bring her back at all costs. He would probably arrange to marry her to save her good name—but Ella loved Pete, and Vicky could see no way that Ross could alter that.

Her unhappy eyes met Mary's. 'I'm sorry, Vicky,' Mary said in a low voice. 'I guess things didn't work out for you. I still think that if you had married Ross you'd have been happy. Not all marriages are made in heaven, some need a helping hand from us ordinary mortals.'

Vicky swallowed. She looked away from Mary and down at the floor. As long as Mary thought it was Pete that she cared for, there was no harm

done. She could face the future, even if Ross was
successful, and brought Ella back. 'Don't worry,
Mary,' she said lightly. 'I liked Pete, but I didn't
go overboard for him. I only met him once. You
can hardly call that an affair,' she added, still
managing to keep an airy note in her voice.

Mary looked at her. 'That's not what Pete
Noonan put around,' she said. 'According to him,
you'd got a big thing going between you. But I
didn't mean Pete,' she added quietly. 'It's Ross,
isn't it?'

It was Vicky's turn to stare at Mary. Then she
looked down at her hands. 'How did you know?'
she asked in a low voice.

Mary gave a light shrug of her broad shoulders.
'Call it womanly intuition,' she said. 'You didn't
fool me for one minute with that gay chatter of
yours when you came back from Jarra. I knew
something had happened, and when you started
avoiding Ross, and stopped talking about him,
then it was the only thing that made sense. I
thought you were trying to make Ross jealous by
seeing Pete,' she added.

Vicky frowned. 'I only saw Pete once,' she
repeated slowly, and her brow cleared as the
answer came to her. 'Pete was trying to make Ella
jealous,' she explained to Mary. 'He's been courting her for about a year, and Ella was terrified her
father would find out.' She sighed. 'I suppose Pete
laid it on with a trowel, using me as a cover-up,
and to put Ella's father off the scent.' She hesitated.
'As for me—well, I had my own reasons for falling

in with his schemes.' Her eyes met Mary's. 'And it wasn't a plan to make Ross jealous,' she added meaningly.

Mary's brows lifted as she digested this news. Then she said thoughtfully, 'Well, that makes more sense than the drivel bandied around about you and Pete. We had the devil of a job keeping your father from hearing the gossip. Being confined to the office made it a lot easier for us,' she added. 'You know how the hands talk.' She looked at Vicky. 'How did you find out about Ella and Pete?' she asked.

Vicky gave a wry smile. 'Ella told me herself. She was on the warpath,' she said. 'Told me in no uncertain terms to keep to my own backyard. She also told me Pete was only stirring things up to make her make up her mind about marrying him.'

Mary considered this for a moment, but it was plain that she was having trouble coming to terms with the news. 'Ella might have been doing a little stirring on her own account, have you thought of that?' she asked Vicky.

'I don't see——' began Vicky, then light dawned and she felt a stab of pain in her heart region. 'You mean—all the time——?' she couldn't go on.

Mary nodded. 'It makes a lot more sense than Ella falling for Pete Noonan. She probably only egged him on to give Ross a push in the right direction. Your going out with Pete released Ross from his obligation to you. She must have been a trifle disappointed when he didn't beat a path to her doorway,' she added significantly.

A haze of misery descended over Vicky. It was feasible, too feasible, and was very probably the truth.

When Mary got up a few minutes later to start the dinner, Vicky knew a sense of release. Her world had been turned upside down by a few words from Mary, whose outlook was that much more acute than Vicky's. She had seen what Vicky had failed to see, although sense had told her at the very beginning of the matter that Ella was too sensible to fall for Pete Noonan. Handsome as he was, the old saying of 'handsome is as handsome does' might well apply in his case.

She went over her interview with Ella the day she had come to see her at Jarra. Could she have been acting a part? A part so convincing as to completely fool Vicky? Vicky shook her head. She knew that she was inexperienced in the wiles of love, but somehow she could not see what Ella had to gain by lying to her. Surely it was to her benefit to keep quiet about her feelings for Pete? Unless jealousy drove her to act as she had, she had no reason otherwise to declare her interest.

Her thoughts raced on. What if she had been stringing Pete along in the hope of bringing Ross to heel? Wouldn't the fact that Pete had turned elsewhere for solace bring about such a furious reaction? She shook her head wearily. That was stupid. How could she make Ross jealous if he didn't know about her and Pete? No one knew, it was pointless.

Vicky's head ached. She was getting nowhere

fast. Nothing made sense any more. There was one
fact that could not be denied: Ross loved Ella.
Mary had been right in that, and Vicky should have
been content with that. It was what she had suspected for a long time—only Ella loved Pete. No
matter what Mary had said, she still believed that
to be the truth. There would be precious little happiness for either Ross or Vicky in the future.

She tried to imagine what would happen when
Ross caught up with them. That he would, she had
no doubt at all, and what he would say to Ella to
make her change her mind and return with him.
Would he tell her that he loved her and that he
would marry her?

Her breath caught in a sob. Ross could be very
convincing when he set his mind to it. He didn't
believe in failure. She closed her eyes. Ella was no
different from any other girl—how could she refuse
him? Would her love for Pete stand firm against
such overwhelming odds? To be Ross's wife, with
all the benefits and wealth that included. Vicky saw
Ella's expression again, as she spoke of the diffi-
culties ahead of her and Pete. It was those difficul-
ties that had made her hover on the brink for so
long. In love she might be, but she was sensible
enough to know that you cannot live on love
alone.

Yes, Ella would come back with Ross. Vicky was
convinced of it.

CHAPTER TEN

As no news was expected for the rest of that day, Vicky tried to put the whole thing out of her mind, but this proved impossible. What with her father's and Jake and Mary's comments during dinner that evening, going over the news and what George Waden's reaction would be, her own unhappy musings were not allowed to sink into oblivion.

The following morning, Vicky tried to put a brave face on things. She even managed to eat her breakfast and carry out her normal tasks, although inside her there was a great yawning gap of loss, and that which might have been had things been different.

As the morning hours slipped away, the tension inside her mounted, and was intensified each time she saw Mary glance at the clock on the window ledge of the kitchen and could gauge her thoughts. Surely they would hear something soon?

Each time the telephone rang, Vicky would steel herself for the news of Ross and Ella's arrival back at Albury, but the calls turned out to be routine ones that concerned the running of the station, and she would have to force herself to relax again.

By eleven-thirty, Vicky could bear the suspense no longer. She knew what the news would be, but had not the courage to be present when it came through. Had Mary not known that she loved Ross, things would have been easier for her. Somehow she would have bluffed her way through, but Mary did know, and that was ten times worse for Vicky.

'Want anything in town?' she asked Mary, deciding to take the coward's way out and make herself scarce.

Mary's soft, understanding reply of, 'Not that I can think of, but you might pick up some magazines for me,' said more than any words of sympathy, telling Vicky that she knew how she felt.

Within a few minutes Vicky was on her way, only relaxing as the car headed towards the boundary gates. She didn't particularly want to go into town, but it was as good an excuse as any other, and would certainly take her out of the vicinity until late that afternoon.

In the event, Vicky was glad that she had stuck to her plan of visiting the town, because she ran into Aunt May in the main street, and accepted her offer of having lunch with her at a nearby café.

While she listened to Aunt May's light conversation, and how life was treating her, which by all accounts was very well, Vicky found herself having to suppress a smile at the half-forgotten way that she would dodge from one subject to another—a habit that used to infuriate her father in the old days. He would declare after she had gone that it was like taking a ride on a roller-coaster, you got breathless trying to catch up with the flow of words.

They were doing very nicely when Aunt May suddenly brought up the subject Vicky was trying to forget. 'Is it true you're not going to marry Ross?' she demanded, and as was her way, went on to answer her own question. 'I said it was all a malicious rumour put about by hopeful mothers,' she declared roundly, 'and so I told Bill. Really! some folk have nothing better to do than to make up stories—it's wishful thinking, that's all!'

It took a while for Vicky to get the message that it was not a rumour through to her, and just as long for Aunt May to take it in. Even then, she didn't believe it. 'Nonsense!' she said firmly, and patted Vicky's hand. 'It will work out, you'll see,' she added confidentially.

At this point Vicky gave up. She did not feel equal to the task of dissuading her aunt. She would hear the news of Ross's marriage to Ella soon enough, and she changed the subject by asking her if the flat above the shop was still empty, and having received confirmation of this, then told her of her plan to take some sort of a job, and could she use the flat while she looked around for something?

The news flummoxed Aunt May for a second, but she rallied well. 'Are you sure you want a job?' she asked, and for once, waited for Vicky's answer.

On assuring her that she did want a job, Aunt May said, 'No need to look around. Come into the shop with me. It will be company for me. I've been thinking of getting someone in, but you know how it is, I didn't fancy strangers.'

Vicky thanked her warmly and accepted without hesitation. She would have accepted a road sweeping job at that particular time in her life—she so badly needed something to do that was different and would take her mind off her troubles.

With that settled and a starting date given, in a week's time, to give Aunt May time to clear out the flat, and Aunt May refusing to hear of Vicky giving some assistance, Vicky felt that at last she was getting a break, and was even able to face going back to Dale's Creek. She had got a job, and somewhere to live. What was better, she was being given a breathing space, and above all this, her privacy.

Mary would understand, she thought after she had taken leave of her aunt, and would be a useful ally in persuading her father not to put up any opposition.

The thought of Mary reminded her to get the magazines, and after she had made the purchase she started back for home.

It was four o'clock by the time Vicky reached the boundaries of Dale's Creek, and she automatically slowed down her mileage rate, loath to go back into the homestead, where by now some news must have got through.

Mary was in the kitchen preparing yet another meal, and smiled at Vicky as she wandered into the kitchen. There was no need to ask the question that Vicky dreaded the answer to, for Mary said quietly, 'They're back—got home around two-ish.

Mr Waden's coming back by plane. Ross said it was a pity that he had to hear about it, but Mrs Richards left a message for him at his hotel before she called Ross.'

Vicky absentmindedly picked up a few of the fresh peas waiting to be put into the pan and slowly chewed them, and would have reached for more had not Mary whisked the bowl away quickly. 'Anything I can do?' Vicky asked dully, and at Mary's reply that all was in hand, and had she remembered to bring her magazines? to which Vicky replied 'yes', she went to get them for her.

As she got the magazines out of the car, Vicky was not aware of her actions. All she could hear was Mary's quiet, 'They're back' statement. The words should not have given her quite such a blow as they had, and until that moment she had not realised how much she had been hoping for a miracle. Ross had succeeded in persuading Ella to marry him, just as she had thought he would.

So much for romance! she thought bitterly, as she went back into the homestead, and she felt sorry for Pete, who must be feeling pretty sick right now. Not only was he out of a job, but out of luck in love as well.

After dinner that evening, Vicky's father and Jake settled down to a game of cards, and Vicky and Mary got out their knitting, but in spite of these outward activities, there was a hush of expectancy in the room.

No more news had come from Albury, but they all knew of George Waden's return, but what had

ensued since then was only known by the partici-
pants in the affair, and it was highly unlikely that
any more news would be forthcoming until things
were settled.

To Vicky's way of thinking, this meant Ross and
Ella's marriage in the very near future, and in an
effort to put this out of her mind, she told Mary of
her meeting with Aunt May, and how she had been
offered a job in the shop, plus accommodation, and
that she had accepted the offer.

Normally this news would have caused a furore
from her father and a lift of the brows from Mary,
but they were both so immersed in the drama that
they envisaged taking place at Albury that it hardly
caused a ripple of interest, and Vicky, getting over
her first annoyance at the sudden loss of interest in
her affairs, knew a sense of relief. She had told
them, and with a little luck she should meet no
opposition.

When the phone rang, there was nearly a collision at the door as Mary and her father went to
answer it, and Gordon Dale won the race. A few
minutes later he came back into the room and
shook his head at the hopeful enquiring looks from
Mary and Jake. 'Only Jeff ringing in to say he's
back from town,' he said regretfully.

The clear sound of a motor in the distance and
heading their way sent Gordon Dale to the
window, although by now it was quite dark, and
as it neared the homestead, Vicky, recognising the
heavy throb of Ross's Land Rover, gathered up
her knitting with efficient speed and muttering

something about getting them some coffee, made her escape towards the kitchen to avoid meeting Ross.

It would be better for all concerned if she were out of the way, she thought, for she was certain that she knew the reason for Ross's call—not that he would come out with it in front of Mary and Jake, but he would take her father through to the office for a private chat.

Ross was a stickler for doing the right thing. He would feel that he owed Vicky's father an explanation in the face of his coming engagement to Ella.

Vicky sighed as she made a half-hearted attempt to get the coffee on. It was all so unnecessary. Her father was well aware by now that the old agreement no longer stood, and she hoped that he wouldn't make things difficult for Ross.

She heard the car door slam, and then the front door open and the sound of voices in the hall, but she could not hear what was said.

The next minute she quite clearly heard Ross growl, 'Where is she?' and before she could finish filling up the percolator, a task she had belatedly begun to give herself something to do, his large form stood framing the kitchen door.

Her startled glance went from his blazing eyes to her father's perplexed expression as he stood behind Ross. 'How's George taking it, Ross?' asked her father, unable to work out why Ross should wish to see Vicky before imparting the news they were all waiting to hear.

'Later, Gordon,' Ross said grimly, and strode

into the kitchen, firmly closing the door behind him and leaving her father on the other side of the door.

Vicky had a nasty feeling that she was about to be blamed for the whole thing. Ella had told him of her co-operation in keeping silent, no doubt. Her eyes met Ross's furious ones. She was not afraid of him. She had kept her word to Ella and would do so again in the same circumstances.

'Got a bit of explaining to do, haven't you?' Ross asked in a silky voice, planting his feet apart and folding his arms over his chest in an attitude that told Vicky that she was going nowhere until he had finished with her.

'I don't know what you're talking about,' Vicky lied. She did not know how much Ella had told him, and it would be asking for trouble to volunteer more than was necessary. Her eyes warily watched him as she tried to work out why he was so furious with her. No harm had been done. He'd got what he wanted, hadn't he? Why should he take this attitude towards her? He ought to be thanking her, not berating her!

'I'm trying to keep my hands off you,' he said grimly. 'Any more of the innocent line and I'll give you the hiding I've been wanting to give you for the last twenty-four hours. How the devil do you think I felt when I caught up with that precious pair?' he demanded furiously. 'If it hadn't been for Ella I would have made a first class fool of myself—as it was, she only just stopped me from altering Noonan's features.'

Vicky stared at him and blinked hard. What on earth was he on about? Apparently he hadn't hurt Pete, and that was something. Losing Ella must have been hard enough without requiring first aid, too, she thought.

To give herself time to give a suitable answer, she switched on the connection to the percolator. 'Leave that!' shouted Ross.

Vicky reluctantly did as she was told and turned back to face him. 'Because I knew about Pete and Ella?' she asked quietly. 'Is that what you mean?'

Ross drew in a deep breath as if praying for patience. 'That,' he said softly, 'and a few other things, such as the big affair you were supposed to be having with Noonan.'

Vicky blinked again, then remembered what Mary had said about the gossip. 'Oh, that,' she said simply. 'I guess that was something Pete put around,' and not liking the look in Ross's eyes, she added hastily, 'You did say he had an ulterior motive, didn't you?' hating both Ross and Ella. So she was being blamed, she thought bitterly. Even though he had got what he wanted, he still hadn't been able to resist having a go at her. She wished miserably that she had had an affair with Pete—not that it was any of this hateful man's business. 'What right had you to interfere, anyway?' she demanded furiously, speaking her thoughts aloud.

'Squatter's rights!' he fairly shouted at her. 'I should have used them weeks ago, and by heaven, I'm going to use them now!'

Vicky stared at him, her eyes widening as she

tried to come to terms with this extraordinary statement. She knew what squatter's rights were well enough, but for the life of her she couldn't see what they had to do with her.

'Think about it,' Ross advised her grimly. 'As for Noonan's motive, how the hell was I to know that you were part of the conspiracy? I only knew that Noonan had taken what belonged to me, and what was more, had deliberately used you as a cover-up, and no way was he going to get away with that. Ella was welcome to him after I'd finished with him,' he added grimly.

Vicky stood rooted to the spot, her heart was thudding painfully against her ribs. Her confused mind tried to make sense of what Ross was saying. He had said that she belonged to him—that Ella was welcome to Pete—He'd only gone after them because of her, not because he loved Ella!

A dawning sense of wonder filled her being and crept into her eyes, but she wouldn't let herself believe—not yet. She couldn't bear it if she were wrong.

'How did you get Ella to come back?' she asked, quickly changing the subject.

Ross's eyes narrowed as he acknowledged her tactic. 'Want some leeway, do you?' he queried silkily, 'or just wanting to know what happened to Noonan?' he asked dangerously.

Vicky managed to give a light shrug of her shoulders. 'I asked about Ella,' she said coldly.

Ross subjected her to a bright blue stare. 'That's just as well. We're having no more nonsense in that direction,' he warned her.

'Noonan came back with her,' he added, and
went on to tell Vicky what happened when he
caught up with them. 'They hadn't got as far as I
thought they would have got,' he said. 'Noonan's
old crock had broken down and they were trying
to hitch a lift. When things had got straightened
out,' he said, giving Vicky a meaning look, 'I made
them see sense. They'd nowhere to go, no prospects
of a job for Noonan, only a slight chance of a job
in Mildura.' He gave a grimace. 'George Waden's
a hard man, and he's taken it hard, but he'll swallow his pride rather than see Ella living as a
gypsy—that much is for sure. When he's calmed
down a bit, I'll offer Noonan a job on the station.
At least they'll have a roof over their heads. I can't
see George making any special provision in that
line and would expect them to live at Albury with
him. That might work later, but not now. He's got
to get used to the idea first.'

Vicky's fine eyes glowed as they met Ross's blue
ones. 'Thank you for that,' she said quietly.

Ross gave a grimace. 'It's more than they deserve,' he said firmly. 'Noonan, anyway, after the
hell he'd put me through these last few weeks.
From the rumours that were being put around I
wouldn't have been surprised if it had been you
who'd skipped off with him.'

Vicky's eyes fell to the floor; she found it impossible to look at him. She sensed that he was still
angry with her, but whether it was love or pride,
she wasn't sure. It could have been the latter so

easily. 'And now?' she murmured in a low voice, so low that only Ross's sharp hearing caught it and the inflection in it, that said so much yet so little.

'Now,' said Ross, striding over to her with slow purpose in his stride, 'you're marrying me as soon as I can get a licence. You've had as much leeway as I'm prepared to give you,' and he jerked her into his arms, kissing her with a force that lived up to his words.

After a short interval, they took pity on the other members of the household, whose patience by now must be wearing thin as they waited for news.

Vicky heard Ross repeat what he had told her earlier about Pete Noonan and Ella's return to Albury, going over the whole of it for the others. There was no need to give their news; Ross's firm hold on her waist as she stood beside him said all that was necessary.

It was as if nothing had happened, Vicky thought wonderingly. Here was Ross as he used to be in the old days, spending an evening with them and catching up on local gossip, yet everything had happened. She had only to catch a certain look in his eyes each time he looked her way that assured her of this, and that look had never been there before.

Womanlike, she wanted to know when he had fallen in love with her, for she was certain that although he had intended to marry her, his former approach to the marriage had been anything but a romantic one. Love was overrated, was the expression he had used when she had remonstrated that their feelings for each other were not exactly compatible to marriage.

With a tact that was almost embarrassing, Mary and Jake took themselves off on various excuses, and shortly afterwards Vicky's father, after receiving a few pointed looks from Ross, finally got the message and wandered out to his study.

The minute they were alone Ross swung her into his arms again. 'You're still not sure of me, are you?' he asked her half teasingly, yet seriously.

Vicky raised her brows at this. She ought to have known Ross missed nothing where she was concerned. He had seen those slightly perplexed looks she had thrown him when she thought his attention was elsewhere. 'It's the new you,' she said after a moment's thought, and then cuddled closer to him. 'Not that I'm complaining,' she said softly. 'It's just that it's going to take me some time to get used to it!'

'The woman's never satisfied,' he said with a twinkle in his eye. 'I guess I asked for all I got,' he added with a rueful grin. 'A mite too sure of myself, wasn't I? It took a few backhanders from you to knock me off my pedestal! I'd never felt so damned helpless in all my life when you took up with Pete—or so I thought. And I had to stand by and do nothing. As you so bluntly pointed out that day, it was your choice.' He shook his head slowly. 'There was something else you'd pointed out too. I'd never seen myself in the role of bully before, and there was some truth in what you said.'

His hand cupped her chin and made her look up at him. 'I'd got so used to thinking of you as my girl I simply didn't believe you when you said you weren't going to marry me. When it did finally sink in, I called myself all kinds of a fool for letting you off the hook. I should have gone ahead and named the day. That was my thinking before you gave me my marching orders.' His hand tightened a little as he gave her an affectionate squeeze. 'After that, I had to sit back and do some hard thinking. I realised then how much I'd taken you for granted, and a lot of other things as well,' he added slowly.

Vicky looked up at him, her eyes shining with the light that only love can give. 'I thought you only wanted to marry me because of the agreement,' she said. 'Even your lessons on flirtation didn't alter that. You showed no sign of enjoying them,' she teased him lovingly. 'You gave me no clue whatsoever.'

Ross's white teeth gleamed in a wicked grin. 'I learnt a bit myself that night,' he said. 'I found out that I loved you. I also realised that I was going to have a job convincing you that we should marry. I could have worn you down,' he added, as he traced the outline of her soft mouth with a loving finger. 'I hit the jackpot at the first showing, didn't I?' he reminded her, rather cruelly to Vicky's way of thinking, but she forgave him. Then his expression sobered. 'If you were shaken by the experience, so was I. I meant what I said about taking a leisurely walk down the aisle. I also knew that I was being unfair to you, taking advantage of you, if you like.

I was almost sure that you felt the same way about me as I did you, but I had to keep my distance until the penny dropped. You were too busy seeing me as the boy next door, weren't you, rather than a husband,' he added softly. 'By the way, when did the penny drop?' he asked with a twinkle in his eye.

'The same time as yours did,' Vicky replied with a grin. 'Well, perhaps not right then. Pete——' she hesitated as she felt Ross stiffen at the name. 'Oh, he behaved himself,' she added quickly, and gave him a swift sideways look. 'Well, Pete did give me a peck,' she admitted, 'before I left him that night. I hadn't expected it, and I think I was a bit shocked, but there was something else that I couldn't put my finger on until I'd given it a lot of thought. I found that I hadn't liked the kiss—I mean peck,' she amended hastily on seeing a spark in Ross's eye. 'Then I suddenly realised why I hadn't wanted him to kiss me,' she said dreamily, 'and I knew then that you were the only one for me.'

Ross held her away from him and looked deeply into her eyes. 'Why the devil didn't you say so, then?' he demanded.

Vicky sighed and laid her head against his strong shoulder. 'Because I thought you were in love with Ella,' she said quietly. 'Ella hadn't married, and I thought,' she looked up at him. 'You used to like her, didn't you?' she added. 'And she's so lovely——' her voice trailed off.

Ross's arms enclosed her in a fierce embrace.

'That was when I was about eighteen,' he said in an amused voice. 'Ella's all right, but she's not my type. I like them soft and cuddly,' he added appreciatively as Vicky nestled up against him.

'And so,' went on Vicky, in a small voice, 'when you went after Ella and Pete, I—we—Mary and I thought that it was Ella you wanted.'

'Where does Mary come into it?' Ross asked in amusement.

'Oh, she'd guessed that I'd fallen in love with you,' Vicky explained. 'I was so anxious to avoid you, you see, after I came back from Jarra. You seemed to be avoiding me,' she added accusingly.

Ross's lips roamed her forehead. 'I had to,' he said ruefully. 'You'd more or less told me to keep away from you, and that you preferred Pete,' and he gave her a little shake.

'Oh, dear, what a mess we made of things!' Vicky sighed.

'We?' queried Ross, one autocratic brow raised.

'We,' confirmed Vicky firmly. 'I know I was stupid, but it only wanted three little words from you and everything would have been fine. You only had to say, "I love you" instead of making me feel like an unwanted legacy you'd been landed with,' she accused him gently.

'Aren't you forgetting a few things?' Ross asked in a teasing manner. 'Such as being given the appropriate moment for such tender communications? I seem to recall being accused of giving you a—"bear-hug", wasn't it? Let alone the accusation of having no time for romance!'

Vicky grinned. 'And you told me to forget marriage—with you, anyway. Told me that you wanted a helpmate and not someone——'

Ross's lips effectively cut off the rest of her complaint.

A little while later, he said huskily, 'Now do you see what I meant by claiming squatter's rights on you? I'm in possession, and I'm staying in possession!'

Vicky did see. She also saw that she was the happiest girl in the whole wide world!

AUSTRALIA'S NATIONAL DESSERT

When the famous Russian ballerina Anna Pavlova visited Australia in the early part of this century, the chef at her Sydney hotel served her a new dessert, which he named after her and which has since become an Australian national dish.

To make pavlova you need:

    waxed paper
    4 egg whites, room temperature
    1/4 tsp. salt
    1/4 tsp. cream of tartar
    1 cup fine white sugar
    2 cups sweetened whipped cream
    3 cups fruit of your choice

Preheat oven to 250°F. (130°C.). Line a cookie sheet with waxed paper and grease lightly, then draw an 8-inch-diameter circle in middle of sheet. In a bowl beat egg whites until foamy, then add salt and cream of tartar. Continue to beat until stiff glossy peaks form. Add sugar gradually and beat for 2 minutes. Place half of meringue in circle, then spread and flatten to circle's edges with back of a metal spoon. With a pastry tube, pipe remaining meringue around edge of circle, building sides to a height of 4 inches and leaving a large hollow in center. Place in oven and bake for 1 1/2 hours; take care not to let the "shell" become too brown. Turn off oven, open door and allow shell to sit for five minutes. Remove from oven, transfer to a cooling tray and let stand until thoroughly cooled. Remove waxed paper, transfer to a serving plate and fill with whipped cream and fruit.